LARRAMEE'S
RANCH

1

TOM HOLDEN lay where he had fallen, with his head against the wall and his body sprawled across the floor. A nail had clipped the skin from his forehead, and for the time, with the trickle of crimson, and the deathly pallor which the shock of the blow had given to him, he looked awful enough. So that his mother, though she dared not come to him, cowered and clasped her hands before her face and moaned: "Oh, God, have mercy! Cousin Joe Curtis, you've killed him!"

Cousin Joe took one long stride forward to make sure that the dullness of the open eyes was simply that of a stunned brain and not the vacancy of death. When he was satisfied upon this point he boomed at once:

"A darned good thing if I *had* finished him up. But I ain't had no such luck. I didn't hit quite hard enough. Get up, you young good for nothin'!" He seized Tom Holden by the nape of the neck and wrenched him to a sitting position. Then he heaved the youth still higher, and dropped him into a chair.

Tom, having recovered his wits to a certain extent, began to wipe the moisture from his temple and to compose himself. He was about twenty-two years old. At first glance he looked much younger, his skin was so smooth, and there was such a bloom on his cheek; at second glance he looked much older, because there was a long age of wisdom in that eye.

"Now," thundered Cousin Joe Curtis, "maybe that'll help you to open your ears a mite?"

At this, Tom looked up at the big fellow and surveyed him

quietly, thoughtfully. He had taken the glasses from his nose and was polishing them with much care. When he spoke, he was speaking to the woman who still cowered in the corner with a blank, white face.

"Mother," said he, "are you badly frightened?"

"Hush, Tom!" she gasped out. "Your cousin, he's talkin' to you, boy!"

"I'll wring his impertinent young neck!" thundered Cousin Joe Curtis. And he banged his fist heavily upon the table. There followed upon this a little silence, during which the wind blew down to the shack the foolish sound of sheep bells, far off, and thin. And three or four cows lowed in unison, but so far and small were they that all of those sounds droned through the room no more loudly than the humming of a bee. However, such silences have a weight, and they bore down now upon Cousin Joe Curtis. He sucked in his sandy mustache and he blew it out again.

"Did you hear me speakin'?" he yelled, a more raving madness coming in his eyes.

"I hear you speaking," said Tom.

"Are you gunna get up and go help your ma wash the dishes? Are you?"

"I think not," said Tom.

Cousin Joe Curtis turned to the mother, who gasped with an agony of apprehension and shrank with both of her hands raised to ward away the blow which was to fall upon the head of her son.

"What am I gunna do to him!" breathed Cousin Joe Curtis, smiling out of the sheer ecstasy of rage. "Oh, what am I gunna do to this here fool?"

"If you're wise," said Tom, "you'll finish me now, because if you don't, I'm rather sure that I'll come back, some day, and finish you!"

The blow which had towered above his head did not fall. After all, when Lilliput insults Hercules, Hercules must needs deal gently. Besides, Cousin Joe was too astonished to have governance over his hands. They fell helplessly at his side.

"These are his books," said Cousin Joe at last. "This here comes out of the books that he reads. I ask you, Judith, is they any good in books? Is they any good in this here brat that you brung into the world? Just tell me that."

"Tommy, Tommy!" stammered his mother. "Come in here with me! Quick! You didn't mean what you said, sure!"

And hastening to the door of the kitchen, with her hands clasped at her breast, she turned her frightened eyes upon the boy again. At this, Tom rose to his feet and shrugged back his shoulders so that he could stand the full of his five feet and seven inches. Even so, he had to cock back his head a little to confront the big fellow who towered above him. One could tell, even without seeing the legs of Tom, which the table covered, that he was lame. Something about his posture, and the way he steadied himself by touching the table with his slim hands, and something in the long-endured pain in his eyes told of that crippled body.

"I'm not going to the kitchen," he said.

"Oh," said Cousin Joe with immense irony. "You ain't goin' there?"

"I'm not."

"Maybe you're too proud? Maybe you're too good, you and your books, to wash the dishes after me and my boys that does the work of honest men and keeps you and your ma from starvin'? Maybe you're too good?"

"I am," said Tom instantly. "I'm too good, Cousin Joe!"

It was another staggerer for Cousin Joe. But while he considered it, he wrapped his hand around the top of a heavy chair and raised it till it quivered in his grasp. "If I was to dress you down with this—" he muttered.

"You won't," answered Tom. "Because you know that it would break me in two. And if I were in bed the rest of my life, there would be an added expense to you. Also," he added slowly, "I think you'd be lynched. Some of the people have their eyes on you. They're watching you very closely."

"Here's gratitude, I say," thundered Cousin Joe, tossing up his great hands until they almost swept the ceiling. "This is what I get for keepin' a useless cripple. Why, I got a mind to grab you by the neck and throw you out!"

"You don't need to. I'm going."

"Where?" sneeringly asked the other. "Where will you go, maybe? How'll you keep yourself?"

"Somewhere where brains count. Which isn't in this house."

"Tom!" cried the mother in new terror.

"Let him talk," snarled out Cousin Joe. "I'm learnin' things about him—and about us. What'll be your line of work, young feller?"

"I have my ideas," answered Tom. "But I'm afraid that you wouldn't understand them." He turned his back on Cousin Joe and went to the woman at the kitchen door. And when he walked, his left leg trailed weakly behind him. He adjusted his glasses. Then he took her face between his pale hands and kissed her.

"I'll be coming back for you, dear," said he, "as soon as I have a place. I'll be coming back for you. Will you try to bear this house until I come back? You don't need to fear that they'll throw you out. They'd have to hire a cook, if they did. And they hate to spend money for that. They'll keep you as a slave. They'll even treat you better after I'm gone. And if they don't—"

He turned back to Cousin Joe, who made a rush at him with a roar, and then paused, because seeing the size of his own hand and the fragility of that body, it occurred to him that the blow might be the last that meager frame would endure. And after all, murder is murder, even in the cattle country. And after all, lynching is lynching in any land!

"And if they don't," said Tom slowly, "they'll regret it with all their heart when I come back for you."

He went to the door, took down his cap which hung on a peg beside it, and stepped out into the sunshine. Beside the door leaned a long, slender staff. This he took up, and with it steadied his weak leg as he walked. When he reached the road he whistled, and at once a brindled pup rushed out and began to leap joyously about him. He pointed down the road with his staff, and the dog plunged away into the distance. Tom hobbled after him.

"Oh," moaned Mrs. Holden, "he's gunna leave us—forever, Cousin Joe!"

She ran to the door and cried out. At this, Tom turned, resting on the staff and on his one strong leg. He waved his cap to her and blew her a kiss. Then he went on.

"Call him—oh, let me go bring him back!" sobbed she.

She would have started out through the doorway, but the large hand of Cousin Joe caught her and held her back.

"Stay where you be," he cautioned her. "Because he ain't gunna go far. By the time he's missed a couple of meals, he'll come back. This is from his readin' of the books. But he'll find that days out in the world ain't turned like the pages of a book. Not by a darned sight."

He began to laugh, until his glance caught on the hobbling form far down the road. Already the boy was at the little bridge which crossed the creek, and now he was beside the copse of scrub cedars.

"It's a fool thing for a lame boy to do," muttered the big man. "I—I dunno that I should ha' hit him like that. I didn't mean to hit that hard. But my foot slipped just as my hand was in the air. You know that, Judith. You don't think the kid is gunna go makin' complaints about me to the neighbors? You don't think that, Judith?" His voice dropped until it was almost lost in the deep hollow of his throat.

"He'll never whine," said the mother sadly. "That ain't his way. He'll never whine. He'll be—"

"He'll be a hero, maybe?" said Cousin Joe sneeringly, looking down at her.

She did not answer, but folded her work-reddened hands in her apron. Tom was already by the scrub cedar thicket, and now he was half lost beyond it, and now he was gone indeed.

"He's just gone down to the village," said the rancher.

But the mother knew much better.

2

BUT WHEN HOLDEN came to the village, he turned and skirted around it through the fields, for he had a deep dislike of the questions which would be showered upon him. Besides, some of the children were sure to be playing about the streets at this time of day, and he was game for the children. They could play a thousand tricks upon him, and dodge away from the reach of that long staff. So he cut through the fields. He did not know just where he was going. And as the wrath deep in his heart settled, it became a chill of despair. The dark of the coming evening made him think of one thing only—that he was walking out to his death!

He put this thought behind him with an effort. And just

then his mind was taken by something else. Doc sighted a rabbit and made for it. The brindle was not much use on the trail of a wolf or even a coyote, but he was a terror to cats and to rabbits. Now he scared up a rabbit and went after it. Away he scurried after the dodging flight of the jack. Off and away they went and vanished in the gloom. But Holden, guessing that they might come back again, sat down to wait. Presently through the dusk came the yipping of the dog again. To the very feet of Holden he chased the rabbit, and the poor little beast leaped in between the legs of the man and crouched there, never guessing that this was the archenemy of all. Holden scooped the rabbit from the very jaws of death, and caught it up under his arm. It lay very still, its ears flattened, its eyes dull with exhaustion and the last paroxysm of terror, and all the while its heart pattered like a rolling drum against the arm of Holden. He felt stronger and bigger, and had become, in an instant, the dispenser of fate to at least one creature in the world. This thought he smiled at, but presently he began to stroke the sleek head of the little wild thing.

Doc, in the meantime, having barked and leaped savagely, was soundly cuffed with the staff and ran to a distance. From that vantage point he waited sadly and challengingly. And when Holden called him, Doc tucked his tail between his legs and ran away. After all, this was a turn against nature—for man or any other creature to take into protection that staff of life, the rabbit!

Holden watched the brindle depart with another sigh. For, after all, Doc was something like company, even though very poor company at that. And in the next hollow, he turned the rabbit loose. It cowered for an instant—then leaped up and rushed away, bounding high into the air every seventh or eighth jump to make sure that he was not following at its heels, and finally scurrying off into darkness, which was growing fast. Then Holden went on.

It was practically night, now. His way grew more difficult. He thought of the house he had left, of the worn, sad, kind face of his mother, of the familiar kitchen and its familiar smells, of the face of even Cousin Joe Curtis, with a sort of regret. For they were all he had. And something is better than nothing, even if that something be painful. Now he was stumbling over unknown ways. Twice he caught the toe of his

12

trailing left foot on the rough ground and fell heavily forward. When he had circled back on the farther side of town, the parallel tracks of the railroad, passing off into a shining distance, fascinated him. When a train passed, if he chose, here would be a painless and perfect death for him.

He sat down to take this idea into his heart, but at once he remembered his mother. He had made her a promise. He had made a promise to Cousin Joe Curtis, too, and after all he might be given power to execute both. One never could tell in this wonderful world, so full of miracles of one sort and another—at least so the books said!

He stood up and walked slowly down the tracks until he came to the railroad bridge across the gully, and in the heart of the gully, through the trees, he saw the glimmering of a fire. It was like a beckoning hand to Holden. So he clambered down the steep side of the gully with infinite difficulty, his weak leg continually doing the wrong thing, so that once he almost pitched forward into the empty air, with a full fifty feet to fall to the bottom of the ravine. A lucky clutch at a shrub saved him. He clung there for a moment, shuddering; then he went on and came to the edge of the clearing in the center of which the fire burned.

And near the fire simmered the ragged lower half of an old washtub, giving forth a steam filled with the inestimable fragrance of a rich stew. No one was near, so far as the dull eyes of Holden could make out, so he stepped from the shadow of the trees and made toward the fire—and the prize!

Just what he intended to do was not clear in his own mind. Certainly if he stole some of the contents of that tub he stood in the veriest danger of reprisal on the part of the owner of the food. But he had taken only a step or two when an instinct keener than any physical sense told him that he was in danger. He paused and scanned the little dark arena of the clearing more acutely, and as he did so, as though stimulated by his fear, the fire leaped and gave him a glimpse of two things which were enough to have startled him.

For on either side of the clearing, but backed up against the tree, stood a man with a naked revolver in his hand. It seemed to Holden, at first, that they were both facing him, their guns ready, the food in the tin the bait which was to draw in men for murder. But after this gruesome idea had touched his mind, he was aware that they were not looking at him at all, that they seemed even unaware of his coming, for they were facing each other steadily, and now one of them spoke.

"You first, Blinky, you little rat."

"Me first? I'll see you in purgatory before I make the first move. I don't take no charity from a overgrown sap, a big beef, a sow-sided porker like you, Chris Venner!"

There was a growl from Chris Venner. "I'll tear you to bits for this, Blinky!"

"You'll never get them hands near me again, you cheap bum. I'm gunna let a couple of slugs of daylight through where your brain ought to be, and ain't. In your belly—that's where your brain is. That's where you do your thinkin'—with your guts, you hog!"

"Are you ready?" snarled out Venner savagely.

"Ready, damn you!"

The air grew charged with that deadly tenseness of expectation which precedes a violent action. Then the crisp, cool voice of Holden broke in. It was a very pleasant voice. He had a trick of making it carry without raising it, like the ringing tones of a bell which melt through the thickest walls and into the farthest corner of a house.

"This is very good," said he. "I will have two shares of stew to myself. And for nothing!"

His voice came in on them so suddenly, so unexpectedly, so blind had they been to his coming in the depth of their mutual passion, that they grunted, each like a horse under the spur before it leaps.

"Who in the devil is this?" inquired the bull tones of Chris Venner.

"I'll tend to him when I finish you," said Blinky Wickson. "Keep back from that fire, stranger, or by—"

But Holden advanced to the verge of the fire and remained there, with the light bright upon him. Then he leaned and tested the fragrance of the stew at shorter range.

"Tomatoes," he said judicially, aloud. "And beans—canned beans with pork—and chicken—yes, by heaven, there's a good bit of chicken here. I hope you boys both shoot straight!"

The passion to kill is a very violent passion, no doubt; but it is hard for it to hold up its head in the face of certain other things, and one of them is indifference.

"Chris," said Blinky, "gimme a minute's fair play, and

lemme take care of this here young rat. Then I'll come back and tend to you."

"You don't need to ask for fair play," said Chris Venner. "But that kid is a crip. You ain't gunna beat up a one-legger, Blinky?"

"What in the devil is it to you what I do?"

"I'm gunna have the killin' of you, you ferret-faced snake!" bellowed Chris Venner. "That's what I'm gunna have! Leave the kid alone, I say!"

They both advanced, and came to the edge of the circle of the firelight, glowering at each other. And there they saw Holden sitting down by the simmering stew. He had reached into the mess with a tentative pocket knife and now he drew out upon the point of the longest blade a bit of white breast soaked in the richest of gravies. He tasted it, deliberately with the eyes of the two killers fastened upon him.

"Delicious!" said Holden. "Before you murder each other, you really should take my advice—"

Chris Venner suddenly burst into huge-throated laughter that roared and rang through the ravine. He staggered across and dropped by the fire. He tossed his gun aside. And still he thundered forth his laughter. Blinky stood by, a short, wide-shouldered man with a long-featured, narrow-faced head and a venomous small pair of eyes. He glowered from his laughing enemy to the complacent form of Holden as though unable to decide on which he should deliver his attack. Finally he drew back and vented his disgust with an oath.

"Are you quittin'?" he yelled at Chris Venner.

The latter rolled to a sitting position.

"Why, Blinky," he said, "it just beats me, that's all. If it was anybody else—but this here kid talkin' up to you, and to me. I call that funny!"

This gave Blinky a new idea. "Maybe the kid don't know," he said.

He stepped closer and leaned above Holden, and the latter could barely repress a shudder, so malignant, so ugly was the face of the man.

"D'you know, kid, who we are?"

"Do I know?" asked Holden deliberately. "Do you think that I came down here by accident?" And, adjusting his glasses calmly, he stared with much deliberation into the face of the other.

3

LET IT BE said of Blinky Wickson and of Chris Venner that their nerves were of the strongest and the thickest ply, but now they were sufficiently shocked to stare at the eyeglassed youth and then at one another, hardly knowing what to do next. If a small bird flies into the face of a lion, the lion is apt to shrink and blink for a moment. So it was with these two renegades, except that Holden, slender and weak as he was, was not any negligible bird but a man, watching them with a quiet pair of man's eyes. They could feel the power of his thinking. They could follow him as he read their minds, and they were distinctly uncomfortable. When they glanced at one another it was as though they said, mutely: "Who the devil can this person be and how much and what does he know?"

Chris Venner, who was the more outspoken of the pair, put that thought into exactly those words. But, for a reply, Holden thought it was much better to merely smile and let the matter go at that. It is always wiser to prefer the cloudy veiling of a mist to the naked daylight of the truth. That which is understood is too often despised. This quiet smile of Holden struck them with a colder awe.

Here Blinky took sudden command.

"Take a step into the woods, Chris," he said. "This bird thinks that he has something on us. And he's got some of his hired skunks along with him, I guess. You take a look around and see what you can see. I'll keep this baby covered."

While Venner went obediently off into the shadows of the

16

woods, Blinky squatted behind Holden, and without turning his head, Holden sensed the flashing of the firelight on the naked gun in the hand of Wickson. Sitting so close to death, he took up his emotions one by one and examined them, curiously, dispassionately. He was not afraid; he could be sure of that. For all fear seemed to have died in him at the same instant when he was able to rise from the floor to which he had been struck and defy Cousin Joe Curtis. He felt, too, that the stakes which he was risking were pitifully small. Other men had good health, wealth, friends, loved companions to lose in death. But he had nothing except this failing body. A child could overcome him!

Yet what child could do what he had just done? Shake two perfect villains with a few words and make them dread him so much that they forgot everything—forgot the bitter feud which they were about to fight out—forgot the very meal which was so temptingly-near?

At this remembering, Holden dipped into the tin boiler again and brought forth a morsel. There was a half loaf of bread near by. He cut himself a slice of this and proceeded to eat with a calm enjoyment. The danger at his back was a mere relish to his pleasure.

"You're a cool little nervy devil," he heard Blinky muttering.

Chris Venner came back to report that he could sight no one in the brush. Apparently the interloper had come without an escort.

"Maybe," burst out Blinky in a destructive fury, "he's gunna leave here without no escort, too!"

He seized Holden by the shoulder and shook him. And the latter knew that here was a crisis. If he let that rude grip pass unnoticed, he was doomed to pass on to greater and to greater perils. His very death might be only a step away. So he made himself turn without haste upon Blinky Wickson.

"All of this," he said icily, "I'll remember against you, Blinky!"

"You'll remember?" said Blinky sneeringly, growing purple with a sudden and very horrible fury. "Why, you sneakin' little runt, what good'll it do you to remember? You—you ain't even got a gun!"

"And doesn't that show you," said Holden, "that there is nothing for me to be afraid of? If I were not amply protected,

17

do you dream that I would come here and put myself in your power?"

This Blinky considered for a moment of breathtaking silence. "You mean," he said, "that I couldn't sink a thumb in that skinny throat of yours and choke you?"

"Certainly you could do that," said Holden. "But immediately afterward, I believe that you would be burned inch by inch—over a slow fire, Blinky! A very hot fire at that."

There was both indecision and infinite malice in the face of Wickson, and Holden added with much energy and great surprise: "Why, Blinky, don't tell me for a moment that you haven't guessed who I am?"

Such a rank bluff as this invariably must have one of two ends. Either it must ruin the man who attempts it, or it must make him. Either it must infuriate those who hear it, or it must overawe them. As for Chris Venner, his slow brain was quite incapable of following the trail of such an agile conversation. And at a time like this he frankly stopped thinking and looked to the keener wits of Blinky to arrive at a just decision. Blinky wavered for a moment with a black scowl on his forehead, but with his eyes widening. Then the scowl disappeared, or only a suspicious shadow of it remained.

"Sure," said he. "I had an idea. I ain't a fool, partner."

There was a sigh from Chris Venner. "You might have tipped me," said he honestly. "I didn't have no guess what he might be. He didn't look like nothin' much."

"My friends," said Holden generously, "it's quite all right. As a matter of fact, I've been watching your work for quite a while."

"You know what luck we've had?" snapped out Blinky, eager to pin down this odd guest with questions.

Holden bit his lip. But, having assumed omniscience, he could not draw back. He had to continue, and he continued calmly: "Of course I know about your luck."

"Well," snarled out Blinky, "let's hear what that luck is?"

The brain of Tom Holden was working desperately. No cornered fox with a pack of swift-coming hounds behind it, ever turned and twisted and wriggled more furiously. The clothes of these men most certainly indicated poverty. Besides, the clothes could not be indicative of anything while they were roughing it, no matter what they might indicate in a town of any size. But what could have caused the trouble

18

between the pair? Surely, in hard times, men of this caliber would be soldered together by misfortunes, each realizing that the presence of the other made him stronger and more able to stand up against the tricks and the blows of fortune. But in prosperity, they well might quarrel over a division of the spoils.

On that meager hint he spoke. "I'll tell you, boys," said he, and he smiled whimsically upon them. "You both know a devil of a lot that's worth knowing, and you both have used what you know. And right now you have enough coin to furnish both of you a comfortable stake. But the chances before my coming were very great that only one of you would enjoy the money!"

He saw, at once, that he had struck astonishingly close to the mark. Blinky exclaimed in a loud voice. Big Chris Venner contented himself with lumbering around in front so that he could stare at the face of the wise young stranger and study him in the red firelight.

"And who has the money now?" shrilled Blinky.

Where should the money go except into the hands of the cleverer? And who could doubt that the greater mental agility belonged to Blinky?

"Why," said Holden, "you have it, of course. If Venner had it, there would be no fighting over a fair division."

At this the eyes of Blinky turned green.

"You take his part?" he asked.

"You see?" roared Chris. "Nobody that really knows, like this gent does— What did you say that your name was, pal?"

"Let the name go," said Holden, "for the moment. You can call me Tom, if you want."

"You say," said Blinky, "that I ought to split with him fair and equal?"

"I do! That, in fact, is why I came here."

He could not get on with both of these men. One must be his enemy and one his friend. He infinitely preferred the friendship of the larger of the two, huge-limbed, honest-eyed Chris Venner.

"You was intendin' to overlook the way that we split up the coin?" yelled Blinky, furious beyond control. Then with an effort which turned his face purple, he controlled himself. "Well," said he, "when the voting is two to one, I guess that the thing for me is to give in."

He tore out a wallet and tossed it on the ground. It was so fat with riches that it yawned open, instantly, and exposed the thickly wadded sheafs of notes. Even Tom Holden, for all the iron grip which he had on himself, could not help wincing a little and feeling a fire mount into his brain.

"Count it over," said Blinky with simulated disdain. "Count it over. If you think that I'd crook you, Chris, you just count it over, and I'll let you make the split."

"Sure," said Chris. "I'm dog-gone sorry that you ever figgered I was suspicious of you, Blinky. Darned if I didn't always trust you like I'd trust myself, till you got to talkin' sort of queer a while ago while I was cookin' the stew—you sayin' that you had a right to two parts."

"Because I knew where the lay was; I done the lion's share of the work, and I even done some of the blowing, which by rights ought to have been your work!"

Chris Venner had picked up a bit of string, out of which he made a little lariat and began to noose the stones by the fire, until the noose burned in two.

"That was this job," said Chris. "What about the others?"

"This was the job that brought in the kale," said Blinky gloomily.

"I figger that we took just as big chances on the others when—well, we ain't gunna talk ourselves into a heat a'gin."

Chris began to count the coin; Blinky began to eat, voraciously, steadily, with a purpose, one might say, lifting his eyes with every bite and fixing them for a single brilliant flash upon the two piles of currency which began to grow in front of Chris on the ground. He finished his meal, loosened his belt, went to the trickling little stream of water to quench his thirst, and then returned in time to take the counted-and-recounted pile of money which Chris had prepared for him.

"Count it over, and then count over mine," said Chris.

"Besides what you put in your pockets?" asked Blinky sneeringly, filled with malice.

"Blinky, I done that straight. I wouldn't double cross nobody that trusted me. You ought to know that!"

Blinky, with a shrug of the shoulders, shoved his share into a pocket.

"Well, Chris," said he, "we've finished our trail together. So long."

"You ain't aimin' to break loose, Blinky?"

"Why, you thick head, d'you think that I'd stay around with you—after we've had words like these here?" Blinky stared at him, as though overcome by such settled malice. Then he shook his head.

"Well, Blinky," said Chris, "so long. And good luck to you."

Blinky replied with a snarl and disappeared at once into the shadows of the trees on the side of the gulch which was nearest toward the town.

As for Chris Venner, he remained for some time with his wrists crossed in his lap, looking idly at the fire with sad, speculative eyes.

"Some gents," he said at last out of the depths of his thoughts, "have a way of figgering things out all wrong. Between you and me, Tom!"

Holden said nothing; he was too busy with another idea which had just formed in his mind.

"What'll Blinky be doin' now with himself?" asked Chris.

"Can't you guess?"

"Sure. He'll go to town and blow it in about as fast as he made it."

"Not till he has tried to get some more."

"What?"

"Certainly, Chris. He's not yet satisfied."

"I dunno what you mean."

"He's sneaking back to the edge of the clearing right now, Chris, to put a bullet through you and then murder me and take the whole bunch of the money!"

4

First he watched bewilderment wrinkle the brow of big Venner. Then that man of might leaped to his feet with a face gray with concern, as though he saw, in a blinding flow of mental light, all the truth that lay in the words of Tom Holden.

He made a long stride toward the trees, gun in hand. Then

he paused to look back at the little, scrawny figure of the man by the fireside, so diminutive, with the red of the firelight flickering on his big glasses and shining like silver where it glimmered over the prematurely grayed hair at his temples.

Such indifference in the face of danger filled Chris with actual horror. It partook of the demoniacal. But, at the same time, it foretold perfect success to Chris. He was not the brain which conceived, he was simply the striking arm—the messenger of wrath sent forth by this little deity of wisdom and of vengeance which happened to be sitting now in that gully!

All of these things were read by Holden with some clearness in the face of Chris as the latter turned and stared back at him. He waved his hand; and Venner, turning, plunged at once into the woods.

Big though he was, and apparently clumsy, he was at least in part a good woodsman, for though Tom Holden listened acutely for a time, there was not a sound. Deep in the wall of shadows which the copse of trees composed, there was not a murmur to warn him what was happening, but he knew that big Chris Venner was feeling his way carefully ahead, listening, scarce breathing, and he was equally sure that malignant Blinky Wickson was returning to make his kill, sliding like a snake along the ground. As for himself, sitting out there in the open, it made no difference. Better to be killed at once by the firelight, slain with a merciful speed, than to be overtaken and knifed to pieces in the semidarkness of the woods. For he could have fled neither fast enough to take him far nor silently enough to escape detection.

He turned these matters in his mind, saw that he could not escape, and forced himself to take notice of what lay around him. The trees seemed to have grown taller and denser than when he first saw the fire in the clearing. Now a late moon rose, went up through the eastern trees like a climbing flame, and stood on a dark evergreen's tip. While it rested there, a broad-winged bird of the night flew into the circle of white and hung there for a moment with flapping wings, then dipped suddenly away to one side. Had it been flying toward the clearing or away from it?

Then he heard a footstep behind him; then—and this is actual truth—he heard the breathing of a man approaching— a hoarse, irregular breathing. Then were ten seconds of icy dread. Then Chris Venner lumbered into view and sat down cross-legged at the edge of the fire, his head dropped, his face sullen. And he said not a word to tell of his errand. But, methodically, absently, he worked a long-bladed knife into the sand near the fire back and forth, cleaning it. And Holden needed no telling of what was on the blade.

After the knife was put away, Verner drew out a handkerchief wrapped around a small bundle. He turned out the bundle, which was a tall stack of bills. As for the handkerchief, a stain of some sort on it made Venner throw the thing in the flames of the fire. Next he extended the money to Holden.

"Look here," he said, a little quiver of excitement coming into his voice, "this here is yours."

Holden shook his head.

"I'd be a dead man!" said Venner, growing a bit husky with emotion. "Darned if that skunk wouldn't of got me. He was comin' back. I found him slidin' through the woods mighty secret and soft. He was shovin' his gun along ahead of him. Somehow, a gun didn't seem the right sort of thing to fight him with. A gun might miss. I reached for his throat, and when I found that, I put my knife home between his ribs. He spat at me like a cat. Maybe you heard him?"

Holden shrugged his shoulders. "I can't take that money," said he.

"Take half of it, then!"

"Not a penny."

"Then," cried Chris Venner, "I'll throw it in the fire. It's more yours than it is mine!"

"Wait," protested Holden. "I'll take this."

He took a dozen bills from the top of the stack and pushed them into his pocket.

"That's enough!" he insisted, and he would not take any more. So Venner reluctantly pocketed the others, still vowing that they belonged to Holden of right.

Then he broke in softly: "How'd you guess, Tom? How'd you know that he was sneakin' back——"

Holden held up a hand "Never mind that." he said firmly. 'I can't attempt to explain all of these things. You may even wonder, for instance, how I happened to know that you and Blinky were here, tonight?"

"Ain't I been wonderin' about that?" cried Venner. "Wouldn't I give my eyeteeth to find out how you knew and who told you? Tom, who could of told you? Because nobody seen us come. Nobody could of seen us come!"

"Well," said Holden, "I had a way of knowing."

Venner threw up his hands. It was rather unfair to put the whip upon the credulity of such a simple fellow, but it amused Holden to exercise such an influence over this big, hard-faced man with the murder still fresh and reeking on his hands.

"You had a way," said Chris Venner. "Well, I guess that'll do for me. I ain't gonna try to insist on knowin'. Only—you had no way of seein' Blinky turn back through the woods and start his sneak on me!"

Holden shook his head. "Forget about that," he said. "Here we are with a pair of sound skins. That's the thing to keep in mind. The rain'll see the insides of Blinky, and we're still watertight."

"That's it," said the big man.

"Well, Chris, what'll you do with your money; all that money?"

"This here?" He took it all out in a pile in his huge hands and stared down at it. Then he laughed in an embarrassed way.

"Oh, a gent can always find a way of gettin' rid of it."

"I suppose," said Tom, "that's the reason you risked your life to get that stuff. So's you could have a few days of fun spending it?"

At this, Chris Venner looked blankly at him. It was the sort of thought that crosses a man's day as a nightmare crosses his sleep.

"Why," he said, "when a gent is out of work—he's got to do something."

"Blinky was a smart fellow," said Tom.

"Oh, sure. Blinky was pretty famous."

"He had been at the game a long time."

"Since he was a little kid, I've heard him say. A hobo took him away."

"I know. Well, with all of Blinky's brains, he couldn't make enough money and keep it. And he may wait quite a while for a grave."

Chris Venner writhed where he sat. "I guess there's something in that," he said slowly.

24

"Now," said Holden, "a fellow like you, cut out for honest work—"

"Me!"

"Of course. Blinky and fellows like him have been telling you that you're a smart crook and a bad egg. You're not, Chris. You're—" And here Holden paused, wondering how far he could go. "You're a ridiculous failure," he said at length. "They used you because you had courage and you were good-natured—and easily cheated!"

"Which is one way of callin' me a fool!" thundered Chris.

The younger man looked quietly at him. "About such things," he said, "do you think that you are really very bright, Chris?"

He watched the red die from the cheeks of Venner and the fire from his eyes. "I guess you know me," muttered Chris.

"I guess I do—a little."

"Well, then, what ought I do?"

"A fellow like you—a natural cow-puncher, who knows everything about the range and—"

Here Chris leaped to his feet, frightened. "Who are you?" he yelled. "Who's been tellin' you all this about me?" And he actually backed away from his companion. It was all that Holden could do to keep his face straight. Upon what simple things could miracles be built! He had seen a man handle a little bit of string for half a minute, and out of that sight he had gained enough information to stagger the very wits of the competent, mature man who had used the string as a lariat.

"I dunno that I'd better stay around with you," protested Venner dubiously. "It's sort of—queer! Darn queer!"

"All right," murmured Holden, "you can do as you please. But in the first place, you take my advice."

"Stranger," said Chris in a deep voice, and he even cast a glance solemnly up to the stars as he spoke, "they ain't nothin' this side of purgatory that could keep me from doin' exactly what you told me to do. They ain't nothin' at all! So you just speak out and lemme hear what you got planned up for me!"

"Stop this work," said Tom Holden. "You have a stake now. Buy a ranch; or buy a share in a ranch. Settle down."

"Swiped money don't do no good," suggested Venner.

"You're wrong," said the hypnotist. "That money you have in your hands will do you good if you try to live fair and square. But if you're crooked, it'll ruin you and buy your best friend to cut your throat!"

Chris Venner gasped. "What a man you are!" he said.

"You'll do what I tell you, Venner, or inside of six months, I give you my solemn promise, you'll be as dead a man as our friend yonder in the brush! Do you believe me?"

"Believe you?" gasped out Chris Venner. "Old-timer, I'd rather be caught handlin' lightnin' with my bare hands than to start in and doubt what you tell me is straight! And that's a fact."

5

MAN, TAKE him by and large, is most notably good. But considering him in the individual he is apt to vary a good deal. Boys, taking them by and large, are most notably bad, and considering them as individuals each is apt to be worse than the other. Your benevolent, kind-hearted man, almost beyond doubt was a wolfish little beast of prey as a boy, cunning as a fox, cruel as a cat, fierce as a weasel.

The boys of the town of Larramee were in no wise different from the boys of other regions. They were just as good and they were just as wicked. On this particular occasion they were busied with a peculiarly delightful game. They had a large gray dog with a black face like a mask and black legs— a big, powerful brute whose fluffy tail showed that it was rather more wolf than dog in blood, no matter what it might be by training and habit. This was at their mercy, and they had rendered its trenchant fangs helpless—oh, brutal youngsters!—by winding a stiff twist of bailing wire around its muzzle! They had attached a long rope to the neck of the poor beast. When it attempted to flee, they had only to catch the rope with their hands or jump upon it. Sometimes the strength of the dog overturned them and they tumbled in the dust, to the tune of many cheerful shouts. But always the dog was dragged back into the center of the tormenting circle.

Finally he grew tired of making these desperate rushes

toward the safety of the distance. He was too weary to more than stagger, and the twist of wire which prevented him from opening his mouth caused him to choke and wheeze with the dust. He was very far spent and stood motionless, head down, eyes closed, concentrating all of his attention in a great effort to breathe successfully.

Such inaction would not do. They goaded the poor half-stifled animal with stones and beating sticks, and someone brought out an excellent blacksnake. This was Jud Crogan. One might have said that Jud was too old to have enjoyed such a sport as this. He was fourteen and looked eighteen. He was a man's height, and had a man's spread of shoulders, and a man's more stately bearing. But there were three or four others as old and as big as he in that circle. He ceased to be Jud Crogan. He was only one of a mob. And when he wielded the blacksnake, he yelled with joy to see the dog almost turn inside out in a frantic effort to get away from the flying torment. But the dog was captured and brought back. It made a last frenzied effort. In the greatness of its torture, its humiliation, its rage, it forgot two things—its fear of man and its impotence while that wrap of wire held its muzzle. It rushed at young Crogan and flung itself upon him. Young Jud yelled with fear and tumbled head over heels. He recovered himself at once, however, found that the dog had exhausted itself with the effort, and began to beat its body as it lay in the dust, too weak to rise.

The rest had been the tormenting before the kill. Here was the kill itself. And every boy—every little demon in the lot—all these future good citizens, kind friends, tender husbands, gentle comrades, began to kick, beat and tear the life from the quivering body of the dog which could do no more than emit a choked groan or two. It was suffering so intensely.

Then, into the black of this storm, the lightning struck. It descended first in the likeness of a long and heavy stick upon the red head of the butcher's son. It glanced from the stalwart dome of that youth and crashed upon his well-muscled shoulders so effectually that he bounded high into the air with a screech and leaped away. Half of the others did the same, until they saw that he who had dealt the blow was merely the figure of a dusty little man with great round glasses before his eyes, a frail wisp of a man who supported his weak steps with a long staff—the very staff which had struck this blow.

At this, half of their courage returned. There is nothing that a boy fears more than a man; therefore there is nothing that he more joyously plagues with the wasp stings of his impishness. In an instant they cast out a wing from either flank. And Holden was thinly but securely enveloped. And Jud Crogan, seeing that the enemy was taken in the rear and on both sides, stood his ground dauntlessly over the motionless body of the dog, who was either dead or else was playing possum with the greatest art. Its head was literally white with dust, but still it did not stir. Even its nostrils were coated with the dust. And Jud waved his blacksnake over the body of the victim.

"Stand back from the dog," said Holden in his usual quiet voice.

"Stand back yourself!" cried Jud. Then, ecstatic with the thought that he was defying a grown and matured man, and further fortified by the reflection, which was obviously true, that he was as tall as this man and probably twice as strong, he added furiously: "Stand back yourself, or you'll get what the dog's gettin' now!"

At this, Holden made a slight pause. One might have considered that he was about to retreat, and, in readiness to fall upon him the moment that he indicated the first signs of fear, the whole crowd of boys advanced nearer. But he did not retreat. He held straightforward upon Jud and the blacksnake, and all the circle of the boys held back, waiting, suspicious. There are mysterious powers in the brain of a mature man. A boy can never tell what dreadful danger may be masked behind a comparatively harmless form.

"You," screamed Jud, his voice growing sharply falsetto, "look out what you're doin'!"

He whirled the lash, but the lash did not fall true to its mark. It wavered wildly through the air to one side, because at that very moment Holden, instead of striking with his long cane, thrust the end of it into the face of Jud. It landed on his forehead, where the point made a glancing cut that brought a trickle of blood, and Jud leaped backward with another yell and dropped the whip.

Over the fallen dog leaned Holden, and unwound the fastened wire. There was a streak of blood where its cruel circle had bitten into the working jaws of the beast. And at this release, the closed eyes opened, and showed red, wickedly, as it glanced with snarling lips up to Holden. There never was so poisonous a glance. It would have made another man leap back to save himself. It made the whole circle of the boys gasp. But Holden, being a cripple, could not leap. He was forced to be brave, and in excess of necessity, he dropped his hand and patted the broad top of the wolfish head.

"Besides," yelled someone in defense of their proceedings, "it's a wolf. It ain't a dog!"

Here was the lie given to the last speaker at once. A dusty, red tongue lolled from the mouth of the fallen brute and licked the hand of Holden; and the brushy tail began, pendulously, to sweep the dust. Its breathing was like that of a choked bellows. It was still more than half strangled. And it closed its eyes at once, concentrating all its energies to recover the lost wind.

"Who owns this dog?" asked Holden.

"Nobody," came the answer. "Most like, it's a sheep killer. It acts like a wolf."

Jud Crogan took back the leadership by right of his wound. He advanced to the front rank and shook his left fist. His right hand was fixed on the butt of a borrowed revolver at his belt.

"Stan' back from that wolf!" he yelled. "That's ours. It ain't yours. Stan' back from it."

The red trickled down his nose as he spoke, and the wound in his forehead stung and ached, and this action proved that Jud would be a very brave man, though perhaps a little of a bully, when he grew up. He had a face blotched with red and with white. He was ready to do a murder. He was also ready to cry. And the other boys gasped with joy and with terror.

"Very well," said Holden. "I see that you and I are to have trouble. But I advise you to keep back. You see that this—wolf—as you call it, doesn't like you!"

The big gray dog with its face like a black mask had indeed risen at the approach of its archenemy. The great welts which the whip in Jud's hands had made rounded its body with circles of fire. And now, already more than half recovered from its beating and its exhaustion, it crowded in front of Holden, backing against his legs, only waiting for a word from him to hurl itself at the throat of their mutual foe, and determined with or without a command to keep him from the attack of his enemy. Holden quieted the dog with a word, and

29

it cast upward to him a look of affection and of trusty comradeship which a thousand words could not have expressed with equal eloquence.

"All right," said Holden. "You and I together, partner!"

"I'll—I'll kill that wolf!" screamed Jud.

"If you draw that gun—" began Holden.

He might have bluffed nine boys out of ten. But Jud was red-eyed with rage. And at the threat, he yanked the gun from its holster and jerked up the muzzle to cover, not the wolf dog, but Holden himself!

"I am a dead man," said Holden to himself, and with that, he swung the staff with all his strength. There was not the slightest hope that his blow could forestall the discharge of the gun. It seemed that the staff had hardly begun to swing when the gun exploded and a bullet went on wasp wings past the ear of Holden and clipped a long gash in the brim of his hat. It seemed a very long time after that—time enough for a second shot, almost—before the staff collided with the head of Jud and tumbled him with a yell in the dust. Then Holden picked up the revolver and swung it in a loose half circle.

"Get out!" he commanded.

But what mere man could actually make boys run? These hurried back a few yards. There they waited. And the gray dog jumping astride over the body of the fallen boy, stood there bristling its mane, slavering with eagerness, but looking toward the man for permission. Holden, shivering with horror, called it off. It came toward him reluctantly, backing up, snarling a deep-throated frenzy of rage at the boy, while Jud coiled his legs under him and came staggering to his feet.

"I'll—I'll—*kill* you!" he shrieked. "Gimme back that gun!"

"You're not old enough to have a gun," said Holden. "Besides, I like the look of this one."

He dropped it into a deep coat pocket. It was too big to disappear, and the heavy butt thrust up and swayed sidewise from the partial concealment.

"It ain't mine," breathed Jud Crogan. "It's my dad's—he'll come and make you *eat* it!"

"Tell him to come," said Holden. "I'll be glad to say to him certain things that I cannot say to you. You're too young to understand them."

"Maybe I ain't done with you yet," answered Jud, and he scooped up a rock from the edge of the road.

Holden was in a quandary. If he discharged the gun, there was not the slightest chance that he could hit the target with it. He had never fired a weapon in all his life! And if he did not fire the weapon, what would come of him, except what had so nearly come to the wolfish dog which was now growling beside him? For all the circle of youngsters was gathering stones, with murmurs and with laughter, ready for the fray.

Here a voice cut in dryly from the side: "You better scatter, you scalawags! You better clear out!"

"Cheese it!" cried one among the youthful vandals. "It's Miss Alexa's Aunt Carrie."

That seemed a name of note among them. They were gone in the twinkling of an eye. And young Tom Holden found himself facing a tall woman with bent shoulders and a lean, ugly face who stood behind the nearest gate, with a pretty garden behind her, and behind the garden a white-faced house with green shutters, and a red roof. It was for all the world like the neat cottage of the fairy tale, and here was the old witch that guarded it with evil.

6

"You'd better come in here and sit down," said the witch.

"I'll be going on, thank you," said Holden.

"Are you afraid of Jud Crogan's father, when he comes for that gun?" asked the witch with a hideous grin.

Holden's dignity made him stiffen. "Certainly not," said he.

"Very well," said the witch. "If you come in, I'll give you tea and toasted muffins and strawberry jam. Besides, there might be a crumb or two for that wolf."

The latter, as though he understood only her last word, shrank closer to the master and snarled viciously.

"What an ugly dog," said the witch. "Come in!" She opened the gate.

"My name," said Tom, tucking his hat under his arm, as he had heard that young men should do, "is Thomas Holden."

31

"Very well, Tom," said the witch, holding her skirts aside from the dusty flanks of the dog as it skulked through. "I'm Aunt Carrie. Wipe your feet on the mat before you go in. My, my! Tom Holden, how'd you come to get all that dust on you?"

She added: "You can take that dog of yours—that sneak—in along with you."

This was the baptism of Sneak, though he knew it not. He required much coaxing before he would consent to enter a human habitation, and when once he was persuaded to go in, he skulked with his tail between his legs and then lay down squarely upon the feet of Tom when the latter was in a chair. There lay the great dog and snarled wickedly whenever the witch came near with tea or food.

It was a very neat little house, furnished with old-fashioned things. Aunt Carrie left the kitchen door open so that she could talk while she prepared the tea. And Holden, looking through, could see her long, ugly arms darting out here and there, while she did many things with amazing speed and prodigious lack of noise. The tea was made and the muffins toasted almost before Holden was well settled in his chair, and at the same time the witch had learned that Mr. Holden had come down from the mountains merely for the sake of travel and to satisfy a certain wanderlust in his heart.

She listened to this brief narrative with certain murmurs which were much akin to grunts. Then she came in again, bearing a great tray. How much she had done in how short a space! There were quantities of muffins piping hot. There were two kinds of jam, strawberry and red currant, there was tea and cream and sugar and butter yellow as gold. Holden ate and ate and ate, while the witch sat crookedly in her chair with her great long head thrust out on her great skinny neck, and her little birdlike eyes blinking at him with intense deliberation. And she ate nothing, but sipped her tea in continual rapid little swallows which did not in the slightest diminish the amount of tea in her cup.

As for Tom Holden, the more he saw of this little house, the more comfortable he observed it to be. The rug in the floor of this room was a brilliant riot of blues and red and deep old golds. There were chairs with odd bits of needlework and tapestry for upholstery. Outside the three windows were three window boxes which carried a bright bit of the garden into the very room, as it were; and since the windows were open, the breeze kept up a continual rustling and whispering through the house and stirred the gay yellow and crimson chintz curtains which framed the windows.

All of these things, these bright and cheerful things, Tom Holden observed while he ate. And at length he could not help asking: "I suppose that your husband is a—"

Then he stopped short and grew very red and stared at the lady hard. For how could he be sure that the witch was married? She did not leave him in doubt.

"I am a single woman," said she, stirring her cup of tea round and round, very fast.

"I'm sorry," said Holden, feeling ridiculously ill at ease.

The frown on the brows of the witch dissolved a little.

"All young men are without tact," she announced gravely. She continued to hold the spoon with three fingers and liberated a long forefinger to point at him. It was an excessively hard and bony finger. And it made the eyes of Holden start a little wider.

"Do you know that that ugly person, Crogan, will be here after you?" she said.

"Who," asked Holden absently, "is Crogan?"

"The boy with the gun—"

"Oh!" said Holden. "Is the father like the son?"

"More," said she with a sort of gloomy joy. "And how will you handle him, young man?"

It began to seem to Holden that the witch had invited him into her house as into a spider's web, to keep him there until Crogan came to execute a vengeance.

"What can he come for?" asked Holden faintly.

"For the gun, for one thing! Of course, you took his revolver away from the boy!"

Holden uneasily shifted in his chair, and so shifting his glance passed through the next open doorway into a little morning room, done in delicate shades which now were all in shadow since the sun had passed to the western side of the house; but a leveled ray of brilliance slipped through the doorway and fell fairly upon the picture of a girl which hung upon the opposite wall, and her blue eyes found Holden and her soft mouth smiled at him. He was transfixed.

Perhaps the witch took his stiffened attitude as a tribute to the dreadful sentence which she had now pronounced, and with a wicked joy she leaned closer toward him above the teacup, leering, and stirring the cup with infinite rapidity, her gaunt forefinger pointing at him all the while. She went on to complete her work: "That's not all, young Mr. Holden. Crogan is a gun fighter. He's a killer. I don't know how fast you can—"

Here she was amazed to see the cripple raise a hand to stop her talk and then rise slowly to his feet where he supported himself on the back of the chair. The great wolf dog rose beside him, and the other fragile hand of Holden was dropped upon the shaggy head of the beast.

"No more of Crogan," he said abruptly. "But who is that?"

"Who is what?" asked the witch, scowling at him, but it was plain by a certain light in her eye that she knew what he was seeing.

"Who is that beauty?" breathed Holden. "Who is that sweet girl?"

He went a little closer, drawn unconsciously forward. Now he went without a staff, even, and his hobbling was a pitiful thing to watch. The big dog, Sneak, walked anxiously beside him.

"Ah," said Holden, as he saw how the shoulders of the picture were dressed. "I understand. This is a picture of some great-aunt of yours, or some grandmother, painted years ago before some wooden-headed lackey with a title married her, and moved to—the colonies! That is it!"

He slunk back to his chair with a fallen head and sank into it.

"Well, well," murmured the witch, "I do believe that you have been looking at my Alexa!"

She did not want to say a pleasant thing, perhaps, to this fellow who was to be destroyed in her presence by Crogan; but it was so pat and so quick on the tongue that it popped out before she was aware.

"I do believe that you have been looking at my Alexa!"

"*Your* Alexa?" cried Holden with an emphasis that made her flush and wince.

"I was her governess for sixteen years," said she.

"But you left?" asked Holden.

"What could I do? Rather than see her married to an old fool of a millionaire, I raised my voice for the first time in that house. I told Mr. Oliphant Larramee what I thought of him and his ideas. After that it was impossible, of course, for me to live in the house."

She dropped her squared shoulders back in the chair.

"She's married, then?" asked Holden softly.

"No matter how much poor Alexa loved me and missed me!" said the witch.

Holden grasped his staff from beside his chair and dashed the point of it against the floor, where it dented out a cruelly deep groove.

"She's married, then?" he thundered.

"God bless me!" gasped out the witch, and stared at the dent in the floor. "Of course she's not married. What I said in her father's presence had an effect on her. She was wakened, I thanked God. That very day, after I left the house at the order of her father—and according to my own inclination— Alexa stood before Oliphant Larramee and used my words to his face." The witch closed her eyes and repeated with infinite joy: "To his very face!"

Something broke in Holden. Joy flooded his face. "You are a very good woman," said he.

"Tush!" said the witch.

"And a very wise woman," said he.

At this she raised her eyebrows, and then squinted at him. "To hear you talk, Mr. Holden, one would think that I had saved her for you." She broke into fierce, sharp laughter. "For you!" she repeated with such a thrust of sarcasm that Holden sat up straighter.

"Well, well!" said he, and gave the wolf dog half a muffin at a bite. That poor brute swallowed the morsel and then looked up in the face of the man with moist eyes of hunger and affection and dumb gratitude.

"I think the dog loves you!" snapped out the witch. She leaned forward to observe more closely. "Dogs are unreasonable beasts!" said she in conclusion. "Now," she added, briskly, "tell me what you meant by adventuring among all those young wolves—I mean, among all those young boys in the street?"

"I?" murmured Holden, fencing for time and much surprised.

"Exactly what I say. Answer me!"

"A mere scattering of youngsters," said Holden with a magnificent gesture.

"Humph!" grunted the witch. "That scattering might have torn you to bits. Wolves—that's what they are. They've killed two of my cats. They ran my poodle to death with a can tied to its tail. They would have slaughtered you without an afterthought. Without a single one!" She added, glaring at him: "And you know it!"

Holden surrendered at once. "I know it," said he.

She struck a bony hand upon a bony knee. "Then why did you do it?"

"The dog, you know—" said Holden faintly.

"Bah!" cried the witch. "They might have torn you limb from limb. They came mighty close to it as it was."

"I suppose they did," sighed Holden.

"You didn't know the dog!"

"Ah—in fact, I suppose that I didn't."

"And you had no weapon with you."

"The staff, you see."

"Rot! They could have stoned you to death from a distance and run away when you tried to catch them."

He flushed and sat straight again. "Perhaps," said Holden coldly.

"Do you mean to tell me that you actually had no gun?"

"Of course I didn't have one. I don't know how to use a gun, anyway, you know. They aren't the slightest use to me for that reason."

"By heavens!" cried the witch. "You did this for the sake of a dog?"

"What else? Of course it was for the poor dog. Eh, boy?"

Sneak licked his hand fondly, in recognition of that tender lowering of the voice which flowed like exquisite music over the brute soul of the dog.

"Nonsense!" shrilled the witch. "It was because you wanted to play the hero! It was because—"

Here a bold knock fell upon the front door and she stopped talking, adding immediately: "Who dares to rap at my front door as loudly as that?"

Deadly premonition rose big and shadowy in the mind of Holden.

"Crogan!" he breathed.

The witch jumped from her chair and the teacup shattered from her hand.

"It must be Crogan," she whispered. "Oh, what can we do? Poor boy! Poor, crippled, motherless boy!"

7

SUCH A BURST of tenderness seemed to Holden like a mockery of reality. He looked at the witch and he looked at her again, and he saw once more the flush of light in her eyes which he had seen there once before as she was thinking of her Alexa. The sun had set. The red afterglow filled up the sky from horizon to horizon; but that light hung like the color of a picture outside the window and very little of it entered the room. There was only the dusk, the beating silence, and the tears in the eyes of Aunt Carrie. She came to him and took his hands.

"I can hide you!" she whispered.

By the fear in her face he knew more exactly just how terrible a creature this Crogan must be. He knew, furthermore, that it was useless to flee to a hiding place. Crogan would hunt for him and find him, and draw him forth by the nape of the neck and carry him forth to the street and beat him in the presence of young Crogan and all the other boys. Holden could hear them now as they gathered thick in the street with a murmuring of voices, some deep and obscure, some bright and high like the talking of birds in the morning. There was no refuge in flight.

Here the great hand of the man at the door beat again, and the house trembled and the floor quivered under the feet of Holden. He grew sick. The face before him was dim with more than the dusk, and something like a prayer formed in his heart.

But the rat must go to face the danger from which running will not carry it away. Holden withdrew himself from the hands of the witch.

"Sit down in the next room," said he.

"Ah," gasped out the witch, "you are going to let him kill you? Child, child, you don't understand! This great beast of a man will crush you, grind you under his feet. He is the king of brutes. There is no man in him."

"Hush!" said Holden, putting his hand on the butt of the heavy revolver. "Women don't understand these matters."

With this, he went to the door and flung it open. Before him, emblazoned by the sunset, was the monster Crogan. He was very huge. He was even larger than Chris Venner had appeared, though this could be merely guessed. The mounds of his shoulder flesh rolled up almost equal to the base of his jaw in height. He had immense long arms like the arms of Blinky Wickson, and the arms of Crogan were like the thighs of a strong man in thickness. He knocked back his hat as Holden appeared. He knocked back his hat so that the hideousness of his face would be apparent and crush the soul of a smaller man.

"You," said Crogan, "are the gent that thrashed my boy Jud, maybe?"

He added, for fear that he had been unfair to one of his own flesh and blood: "You're the gent that hit Jud when he wasn't lookin'?"

The answer of Holden was a miracle of gentleness. "I am the man," said he.

There was a little choked gasp from the dark of the room behind Holden, but Crogan did not hear it. A spasm of rage wrinkled the fleshy face of Crogan. He reached for the butts of his guns. He changed his mind and fingered the haft of a knife. He changed it yet again and balled his great fists, fringed all about with thick red hair.

"You're the one that stole my gun from him, eh?" he remarked.

"I took the gun away from him," said Holden.

"I've licked him," said the father, "for gettin' licked. Now I've come to let him see me get the gun back!"

"You will have it, Mr. Crogan," said Holden.

This mildness brought a green devil into the eyes of Crogan; he saw his prey delivered voluntarily into his grip.

"That'll be one thing," said Crogan. "After I got the gun, they's other things to talk about, and we'll sashay along to them later on. Now lemme have this here gun."

The boys had swarmed to the fence to watch. One and then

another jumped the fence and strode recklessly over the sacred garden of Aunt Carrie to be nearer to the great scene.

"By all means," they heard the gentle voice of the cripple say, "as soon as I understand that you should have it."

"You mean," said Crogan, controlling his wrath, "when I prove that it's mine? I can do that by the notches on the—"

"Not at all," said Holden. "I can let you have the gun just as soon as you prove to me that you know how it should be handled—just so soon as I am convinced that you are not a murdering brute, Crogan!"

No one believed what they heard. Certainly the boys by the fence could not give credence to their ears. Certainly the woman cowering in the dark of the room behind could not believe. As for Crogan, he was staggered and even gave back half a pace. But Holden, striking simply because he knew that his nerve could not hold out much longer under this strain, saw the big man waver back close to him and saw him swell with fury.

"I'm to explain, eh?" said Crogan. "The explainin' that I'll do to you, you—"

Here his voice faltered. Something shoved past the thigh of Holden, and he looked down to the dusty, terrible head of Sneak; all in silence the beast stood there, its lips writhed back from the great fangs, the hate in its eyes, as though it recognized the cruel son in the cruel father. Crogan drew in his breath with a gasp.

"You got a wolf in there with you," said he.

He shrank back to the edge of the steps. Sneak glided two silent strides in pursuit; Crogan leaped backward to the ground. He was too frightened to have sense, even, to lay a hand on a revolver, for the moment.

As for Holden, he saw himself saved by a miracle from destruction, but like most men, he forgot to be grateful to Providence the moment the height of the peril was over. Yet he felt greater mastery, greater content in himself.

He spoke to Sneak, and at his voice the great dog sank on its belly, though it still slavered horribly as it stared up at the fat throat of Crogan. Now the latter regained self-possession enough to jerk out both his Colts, a shimmering long pair of guns, and a gasp of joy and terror ran down the lines of the waiting boys by the fence. They huddled closer to one another, and they grew white, but not one could take his eyes from the exquisite torment of the scene.

"Don't shoot," advised Holden.

"I'll blow the wolf to pieces," said Crogan, "and then I'll fix you, you rat."

He shrank back a little, fascinated by the eyes of the dog. Nothing is so terrible as a dog turned enemy. Crogan tasted in forethought the white teeth sinking through his flesh and grating on his bones.

"If you fire at the dog," said Holden, "you'll probably miss. And even if you wound him, he'll put his teeth in your throat. And even if he missed you, Mr. Crogan, I'll undoubtedly kill you. Do you hear me? I have no desire to murder you, Crogan. In your present condition, with your hands shaking, it would be nothing less than murder to fight with you. Do you see your hands, Crogan?"

This was brutal. Crogan, looking down against his will, saw his big hands trembling and the light shaking along the barrels of the Colts.

"A dog to back you up—a wolf to help you," he gasped out. "What—what—"

Beyond the monster, Holden glimpsed the awestricken faces of the boys, already beginning to read the writing on the wall, already seeing that Crogan, the Terrible, was about to fail. But Holden saw even more. He saw that Crogan had been shocked out of all self-control.

"A dog to back me up? Crogan, do you realize who I am? Do you know me?"

He stepped out upon the little porch. That step revealed his crippled leg. But it revealed, also, a commanding frown upon his forehead and his right hand clasped upon the butt of the big revolver. Crogan's own gun!

"Come back, boy!" commanded Holden.

The wolf dog shrank back, glided behind its new master, and then crouched in the throat of the darkness at the doorway, where its two eyes were bits of phosphorescent light.

"There," said Holden, "I have sent the dog away. You and I are alone."

This was very untrue. The dog from the doorway was even more terrible to poor Crogan's excited imagination than the dog had been when it stood in the full light of the evening.

40

Moreover, he was growing more and more uneasy. He had heard with astonishment how one crippled youth had scattered the ferocious boys of the town before him. Now he began to see reasons why that strange thing had been accomplished. The slender hands, the large, weighty forehead above the slender face, the great, round glasses, the patient eyes—these things which had excited his bitterest scorn at first now wakened in his breast a deep and unreasoning awe. He had been shocked into fear, first, by the nightmare apparition of the wolf dog. But now he was in the condition of one who has already turned his head and begun to flee—even a child could have frightened him away.

And now Holden drew out the Colt. It was a heavy burden to his unmuscled arm. That made no difference. At the full length of his arm he let it hang.

"Until I count five, Crogan," he said. "After that, if you are still in the yard, I'll have to kill you—my man!"

Crogan looked wildly about him. He was neither a fool nor a coward. He was only a bully, and therefore used to taking things in a rush. These delays were deadly things to him. They let the brute out and let the mind in, so to speak. And this was what baffled Crogan. He did not understand mind. It was a foreign substance. It was not in him.

He took one step backward to brace himself, he said in his own mind.

"One!" said Holden.

But just as Crogan took that backward step he heard a little indrawn breath behind him, a breath drawn by many throats. Oh, how many were there to watch, and what if they thought that backward step was in flight? Indeed, worst horror of all, what if he *did* flee?

At this Crogan's forehead was coated with cold water.

"Two!" said the voice from the porch, raised a little and ringing in a strange fashion that went to the very soul of Crogan. "Three!"

"Come down here where—" gasped out Crogan.

"Four!"

"Oh, Lord!" moaned Crogan, and, wheeling on his heel, he fled with the guns through the streets of the town.

Not a head turned to watch his flight, not a voice was raised. Of all the score and a half or two score young and hardy devils by the fence of Aunt Carrie's front yard, not one had an eye for the fall of the great Crogan. But all stared fixedly, through a hush, at the slender form on the porch of Aunt Carrie's house. They saw the light shimmer on the broad glasses of his spectacles; they saw the delicate whiteness of his hand upon the staff, his hand upon the gunbutt. Then love, awe, worship poured across their faces. Crogan had been ever an unsatisfactory hero, for a boy must be able to love where he worships. But now there was a new hero, strange, with a strength immeasurable because inexplicable.

They waited until he disappeared into the darkening house again. Then, as having seen a mysterious, almost a holy thing, they broke up in silence, and in silence they went home.

8

BUT IN THE dark of the house, little Tom Holden slipped into a chair by the window and lay back in it with his eyes closed. The heavy revolver dropped from his hand to the carpet. Sneak came to examine it from end to end, carried it to a distant corner, and then lay down to chew the butt. But this Holden did not heed.

Then Aunt Carrie brought a lighted lamp and set it gently on the table beside him; next she drew the window shade near by, rather hastily.

"How are you feeling now?" she asked.

He opened his eyes and smiled up to her. "A little shaky, still," said he.

She went without a word into the kitchen and returned with a glass of fragrant apple brandy.

"Close your eyes and breathe deep before you drink it," said Aunt Carrie, "and you'll be able to see a whole field of apple blossoms. I know!"

He obeyed.

"It's very strong," said Tom Holden, coughing. "And very good."

She took the glass again and frowned down at him. "Were you *very* scared of him?" she asked at last.

"Terribly!" said Holden with perfect frankness. "I was so frightened that I was sick. I still am—a little. But then, the brandy helps a lot."

She sat down, still holding the glass, and from time to time inhaling the fragrance of its last drops.

"What gave you the strength?" she said.

"I had to brave it out. Otherwise I was lost. I knew that. The brute was written so clearly in his face!"

"Well," said the witch, "if you had failed—"

"That would have been the end of me."

"Do you think he would have killed you?"

"Of course not. But he would have beaten me, with his hands, you know. And when he was through, all the boys would have had their fling at me. And after that—I never should have been much good again as long as I lived. Any child could have made me tremble."

She considered this confession for a long moment, nodding all the time and still frowning at him.

"After all," said she, "I thought that you were very brave, but it seems that you were only afraid of being afraid."

"Exactly."

"There was a moment when I actually thought that you were almost a hero."

"Ridiculous," said Tom Holden. "It was simply an immense bluff."

"Oh," said she, and smiled strangely at him. "But don't keep up the bluff with me!"

"That would be foolish."

"Why so? Because you know that there's nothing to fear in me?"

He shook his head at her. "Some people have eyes that look through things," he said. "You're like that."

"Humph!" said Aunt Carrie. "I suspect you very much of being a shrewd young flatterer, but nevertheless I wish that I could be of some help to you. I've an idea that your father is not taking much interest in you just at present." And she eyed his clothes.

"He died long ago," said Holden.

"And your mother?"

"She can't even help herself, poor dear. That's why I left home—to make a fortune for her, you know."

He took off his glasses and smiled at her, and she almost smiled back!

"Your eyes don't look in the least weak," said she.

"Don't they?"

"Not a whit."

"As a matter of fact, they aren't."

"Then why do you wear glasses, foolish boy?"

"One has to do something for the sake of appearances. Really! These bits of window glass make me look a bit older and more settled, don't you think?" He put them on again and regarded her with a judicial air which made the smile come very, very close to the corners of her mouth.

"You are a queer youngster," said she. "How are you going to make money for your mother?"

"I haven't settled on that," said he.

"Have you any profession?"

"None at all. Besides, professions are much too slow. Poor mother needs happiness quickly."

"You really are fond of her, I see."

"She's a dear thing," said he.

"About this matter of making a fortune. If you have no profession, perhaps you want to try your hand at prospecting or some such matter?"

"Drag my leg over the mountains?" said he with a smile which did not leave his face less sad. "No, no! I could never do such a thing as that, and I know it. I have great limitations, you see!"

He took off the glasses and regarded her gravely. He looked very young with the glasses off.

"You are a boy, really!" said Aunt Carrie.

"I am twenty-two," he protested.

"Well, well! You're a child. Not bad looking with your glasses off. You might marry money, my boy."

"The very thing!" said he. "But, unfortunately, my mind is made up."

"About what?" said she, frowning more darkly than ever.

"Is the lady in the picture—" Here he pointed toward the next room. "Has she much money?"

"The lady of the picture—my Alexa—heavens, boy, what has she to do with this business?"

"I'll be perfectly frank with you. If I do not marry her, I shall never marry anyone!"

He saw the red blood pour over the face of the witch. Then she stamped to the window and jerked up the shade. Night was passing fast across the world. The face of the ground was already velvet black, and the western hills were like cut-out cardboard silhouettes. Between the two highest hills, painted in black also on the last delicate rose of the western sky, there was a great house. Lights showed in some of its windows. More lights were kindled momently and cast splintered yellow rays down into the valley and toward the town.

"Do you see that?" asked the witch.

"It is a lovely place," said he. "Are those poplar trees—that fringing on the hill to the right?"

"I mean the house."

"So do I."

"Young man, Oliphant Larramee lives there!"

"Well, well! I suppose he is rich, then?"

"His father left him a big fortune."

"Inherited money, eh? That's hardly fair!"

"He went to New York, this Oliphant Larramee. He decided to leave the ranch and try his luck where money rolled about more freely."

"And there he lost enough to make him a misanthrope?"

"And there he made so much money that in ten years he decided that he would give up the game. He had more millions than he knew what to do with. He hunted about for a more difficult task still, to give himself something so huge and so hard that wits and money could hardly compass it! And, finally, of all things, he found an island near the coast of South America. All that was on the east side of the island was a terrible jungle full of marshes, snakes, spiders and fevers. All on the west side of the hills of that island was a burning desert on which not even a cactus could be happy and even a lizard considered it hard luck to be among those sands. Well, Oliphant Larramee went down to that island and lived there for fifteen winters."

"What did he do in the summers?" asked Holden.

"He played the race tracks of the world, dined in Paris, heard German music, drank French wines, bought Italian pictures and Spanish castles, was talked about everywhere, and never repeated a word that was said about him. Those are a very few of the things that he did, you flippant young man! But to return to the desert island—"

"That was where luck turned and that was where he lost his millions so that he had to return to the West, I suppose?"

"He drained that jungle; he drew its water through tunnels in the hills and made it stream across the desert. The jungle fevers and the jungle swamps disappeared. The desert became green and gold. And where there had not been a single human soul before there are now thousands."

"Thousands?" said Holden.

"Thousands!" she repeated with emphasis.

"All working for Mr. Larramee, I suppose?"

"Exactly!"

"This is like a fairy story. What brought him back to the West?"

"His daughter, young man!"

"Ah?"

"He did not want to keep her in the tropics. He couldn't live happily there himself without her. He didn't want her in the entanglements of a great city. So he took her to this place. He wants to keep her here until he can find a husband who is good enough for her. In the meantime, he guards her every moment. She is never out of his mind. One reason is because he loves her very dearly. The other reason is that her husband will take with her all of the Larramee millions. Do you understand, young man? Look up there!"

The importance of her gesture made him rise to his feet and stand at the window with the hat crushed against his breast.

"She is like a princess," said Holden softly.

"She is!"

"But you did not tell me—does she love her father very dearly?"

"He is her father. He is also her best friend."

"Ah," said Holden, "for the first time it begins to seem really difficult!"

9

❖

AFTERWARD HE ate supper at the house of Aunt Carrie. And then she followed him to the front door, and down the garden path surrounded by the scent of the green things in the night, and the wet garden mold. At the gate she bade him good night.

"What are you going to do, young man?" she asked him.

"I'm going to stay," said Holden, "near enough to see that house on the hill."

"And keep hope?"

"I suppose that I'll have to do that. I can't help it."

"You are very foolish," said the witch. "She could have a prince, if she wanted him."

"In reputation," said Holden, "princes are apt to be dull fellows. Perhaps she's tired of them all!"

"You're a very pert young man," said the witch, and grinned broadly, because the darkness covered her smile.

"Besides," said Holden, "I have an advantage which no prince could have."

"Humph!" said the witch. "What in the world may that be, if you please?"

"Your kind word in my behalf, and your help."

"You are the most brazen youngster under the sky," said the witch. "What on earth makes you think that *I'll* help you?"

"Because," said he, "I've an idea that you will always have some sympathy for the underdog."

Afterward, when he reached the hotel, he was cold with shame and self-consciousness. He knew that he had said a great many foolish things. He wondered what would be the contempt and the amusement of blue-eyed Alexa if she should ever hear them. So it was a humble Tom Holden who helped himself into the hotel with his staff, with Sneak crowding against his legs and almost toppling him over at every other step—a savagely snarling dog, showing its teeth to every man in the little lobby of the old hotel. Over those men came a hush; and that silence weighed upon Holden. They were rough-handed men—cow-punchers, most of them, and a sprinkling of lumbermen and trappers. He felt their keenly critical eyes upon him. He heard their murmurings to one another.

A fat man in shirt sleeves, his trousers supported by a belt that made a deep dent in his midriff, came to meet him. It was the proprietor.

"You're Crogan's friend, I guess?" said he with a grin, as he shoved the register forward.

"I've met him," said Holden anxiously, and this remark, which in the silence of the room was audible to its farthest end, was greeted with deep-throated, subdued laughter.

Presently he was led up to a room by the proprietor in person, who opened the window and arranged a chair busily. He was plainly anxious for conversation.

"Where might you of come from, Mr. Holden?" he asked.

"Yonder," said Holden, waving obscurely toward half the points of the compass.

"Just travelin', I guess?"

"More or less."

"Maybe you only come in for the dance," suggested the other. Then, taking new note of the crippled leg of his guest, he flushed and began to explain: "What I mean—"

"Never mind," said Holden. "Is there a dance?"

"At the schoolhouse. Everybody is comin' in."

"Including Miss Larramee?"

The host started. "D'you know the Larramees?" he asked anxiously.

"Will she be there?" asked Holden countering.

"I s'pose she will. She ain't so proud of herself as most rich folks might be."

That was enough for Holden. He borrowed a chain from

48

the host and tied Sneak to the leg of the bed. Then he made himself as clean as possible and sallied out for the schoolhouse, staff in hand. It was quite late when he reached it. He found a jam of horses at the hitching racks. He found the buckboards everywhere, and the light through the open door of the schoolhouse showed men and girls idling out of the dance room and into the cool of the night, and late arrivals hurrying in for the next dance. Holden went to the door of the place and looked in. It was at the very end of a dance. He saw the last swirling of the couples. He heard the music crash and die, the talk and the laughter begin, and then the hand clapping in a frantic effort to secure another encore. At last the crowd on the floor began to break up and move in narrow, huddling streams toward the chairs at the edges of the room.

He had searched the whole distant crowd for her. Then, taking him by surprise, she came past, close to the door. It shocked Tom Holden, like something out of a fairy tale turned into flesh and blood. The painter had not flattered. She was childishly small, and her eyes were as blue as the picture, and her smile just the same, half whimsical and half friendly.

A fat man came beside Holden; it was the proprietor of the hotel. "There she is," he said in a hushed, confiding way.

"That's Alexa Larramee," returned Holden.

"You know her then, I guess?"

Holden hardly saw him, hardly heard him. The voice was like a prompting of his own thought, and his answer was a murmured, barely distinct: "She is to be my wife."

He heard the gasp of the host; then he realized what he had said and fled as fast as his staff could help him along into the outer night, and on and on, with the wind of the darkness seeming hot on his burning face. What had he done! And why had he done it? What imp of the perverse had ever brought those words up into this throat? What devil had made him utter them? And where could he flee to hide himself from the ridicule of his fellow men? Why had he done it?

He went back to the hotel. Two cow waddies by the hotel stove tried to hail him and draw him into talk, but he waved them away and labored up the stairs to his room. There Sneak whined a greeting. He dropped down on the floor beside the big dog and buried his face in the ragged, coarse fur of its neck. And he stayed there a long time, shuddering spasmodically as he recalled the question, again and again, and again and again his answer. He tried to put a careless significance on his words, but there was no hope of that. He had said definitely: "She is to be my wife!" And the proprietor had gasped with astonishment. In ten minutes that news must be over the entire town.

Then he thought of the only thing that remained for him to do. He would wait until the first cold gray of the dawn. After that, he would slip down the stairs, leave money for his bill, and strike off down the road. That town of Larramee must never see him again.

He had reached that resolution just as a tap came at the door. Holden dragged himself painfully to his feet and lighted the lamp on the bureau. Then he opened the door and found there a thin young man with a hawk's face. He greeted Holden with a yellow-toothed smile.

"I'm Jefford," said he, "of the Larramee *Tribune*. I'm glad to know you, Mr. Holden."

He took the frail hand of Holden in a strong, moist grip. Then he slid sidewise into the room, extracting a pad of paper from one pocket and a pencil from the other.

"You've given us some of the best copy we've had in months," he said, smiling on Holden. "I wrote up that story myself—how you handled big Crogan. But now it seems that you have bigger news ahead for us. Something about your marriage—"

He poised his pencil.

"Marriage?" frowned Holden.

The other grew abashed. And in his agony of soul, Holden felt a grim pleasure in his first taste of the bully's pleasure. This man feared him—feared him because of what he had done to Crogan. A horse neighed strongly, the ringing, unmistakable wild neigh of a stallion near the hotel.

"There's Doone's Clancy getting ready for tomorrow," said the reporter, grinning. "This is a great week for news. I wish it could be spread out a little!"

"What's Doone's Clancy?" asked Holden, still busy steadying himself and glad to talk of something else.

"He's the blood bay, you know. I guess you've heard about him. The horse that killed Jim Crockett and hurt a lot of others?"

"No."

"Never? He's a bad one. Clancy Doone happened to die the day that colt was foaled. Old Man Doone swears that the bad nature of Clancy went into the colt. So he calls it Clancy. Al Morton is coming all the way from Denver to ride Doone's Clancy in the morning."

He cleared his throat and asked:

"About the marriage with Miss Alexa, do you—"

The first impulse of Holden was to draw out the heavy Colt of Crogan—the gun whose butt was roughened newly by the grinding teeth of Sneak—and send a bullet through the small brain of this news hunter. But he remembered that the whole world knew or would soon know that Mr. Jefford of the Larramee *Tribune* had heard. He controlled himself, though he felt his face grow cold.

"I'm not talking about that," said Holden. "You can ask your questions elsewhere, I suppose?"

"I've been to Mr. Larramee already," said Jefford guilelessly.

Holden closed his eyes and digested the shock.

"Mr. Larramee seemed displeased—frankly, I've never heard a man swear louder or harder. I judge—excuse me, but I judge that the family does not all agree with you and Miss Larramee about—"

"Damnation!" groaned Holden.

"Sir?" said the surprised reporter. "Ah," he added, "I see that I have guessed right. Tell, sir, you know that old adage: The course of true love—"

"Wait!" said Holden, choking. "I want to tell you, Jefford, that if—" He paused, hunting for words.

"As for the announcement," said Jefford, "I assure you that I can make it no more than—er—an interesting hint. I hate bluntness about such matters. I can wield a delicate pen, on my word."

"If a word of this appears," said Holden slowly, "I'll call at your office, Mr. Reporter, and bring my gun with me."

"Mr. Holden!" cried the editor, gliding back toward the doorway.

Then all the fury that had been gathering in Holden, all the rage and the hatred of himself, gathered and broke out into words.

"Are my affairs to be discussed in your rotten sheet? Do you know who I am?"

Mr. Jefford was two-thirds hidden around the corner of the door, but the last phrase held him there, his eyes starting from his head.

"No, sir," he said. "I don't know. It seems to me that I've heard, somewhere, but just a guiding hint, sir."

"You're a fool!" shouted Holden, and he drew the gun out by half of its length.

Mr. Jefford vanished, and flying footfalls echoed back to Holden. Then he closed the door and went miserably to the window. In a little paddock just beneath the window he could see clearly, in the bright mountain starlight, the form of a great horse with a stallion's arched crest and thickly tangled mane. It seemed to feel his eyes even through the dark, for now it tossed up its head with a snort and stood at bay, staring up at him.

Oh, for the speed in that strong body, to carry him to the ends of the world, there to hide himself and his shame forever!

10

HE DREW OUT the bed until the head of it was fairly beside the window. Then, certain that the first morning light could waken him in time for his flight before anything was stirring in the village of Larramee, he lay down to rest, and the last thing he knew was the sniffing of Sneak at his face to make sure that all was well.

But he had done much that day. He had traveled far. His body was exhausted. His mind had sustained a dozen shocks and long torments, and he slept like the dead. When he wakened, the morning light was indeed in the room. It was the blazing sunshine itself which dropped through the window and burned upon his face that wakened him from a dream of rising flames that were consuming him.

Beneath the hotel and outside the window the voices of his dream, taunting demons, turned into the voices of many men. He dressed and then looked out, his mind dazed and sick, only realizing that he had lost his opportunity and that he must spend the whole day in this town, a whole day of questions and agonizing shame.

What he saw below the window only partially took his eye. Around the corral were a full five hundred people, or even more. They were packed around the fence, whitened by the dust which had been raised, and which was still mounting through the air in ghostly columns. Beyond the first ranks of the spectators others sat in saddles, or stood up in buggies and buckboards. One could tell that there had been much commotion. At present there was a lull. The result of the foregoing labors was a saddled horse in the corral, a glorious animal nearly of seventeen hands, his eyes blinded with a sack, his blood-red body darkened with sweat and burnished with the sunshine His feet were braced. The terrible blackness over his eyes paralyzed his efforts for the moment, but he was ready to strike again the moment light came to his assistance. A dozen men were busy about him, some holding ropes attached to his head, others making sure that the cinches were taut, and a final figure in the act of swinging into the saddle.

Holden watched with a melancholy pleasure, remembering what Jefford had said the night before. Here was enough, at last, to wean his thoughts away from his miserable self.

Now Al Morton sat the saddle, fixing his feet more firmly in the stirrups, tugging his hat deeper over his eyes, clutching the reins with a tighter hold, fingering the quirt. In the little silence, free from a single murmur from the crowd, Holden could hear the adventurous rider say quietly: "Well, boys, turn him loose and let's sashay out of this dog-gone corral, if the hoss wants to go."

The last words were torn off short, as the explosion of a gun splits a sentence in two. The bandage had been removed from the eyes of Doone's Clancy, and that mighty animal had flung himself forward and high into the air. He reminded Holden, for the moment, of a gigantic, high-bounding deer.

The three lariats which were attached to the horns of three saddles and managed by as many riders upon expert roping horses, checked the vault and brought Clancy to the earth.

He was transformed from a graceful deer into a fighting-mad demon. He did not attempt to bolt; the area of the corral was plenty for him. With his head stretched straight forth, or tucked between his forelegs, he whipped himself up and down, into tangled knots and out of them again, cakewalking like a proud dancer, then flinging himself back to crush the rider, and snapping his vicious teeth as he landed and turned to his feet. Then he vaulted into the air again and landed upon a single stiffened foreleg with a shock that made the ground tremble and snapped the head of the poor rider violently down against his breast, or heavily across one shoulder.

No one could stand such pounding. Through the thickening dust Holden saw the face of Al Morton turn white with fear and then gray with dizziness.

"Help, boys!" cried Al Morton above the cheering of his friends.

Before help could come, a side twitch of that great body had slipped the rider into the air. He landed sprawling. Clancy lunged in pursuit with flattened ears and gaping mouth —not like a horse, but like a carnivore, an unnatural brute! In the nick of time the three ropes drew taut. Such was the shock of the impact that it tugged all three braced cow ponies forward. Then they dug their feet deeper into the churning dust and held. Al Morton was saved from the reaching teeth, but saved by a scant inch.

They carried Al Morton from the corral; voices shouted and many a bet was paid.

"He's hurt bad!" yelled some one, and the tumult was a little appeased.

Through the quiet that followed: "Forty-eight seconds," said a businesslike fellow. "That's less than Tom Carey lasted in February."

"Tom pulled leather, though."

"So did Al."

"I didn't see it, and I guess I ain't blind. Al rode him straight up."

"Al swore he'd dig him. I didn't see nothing of that."

"Who told you Al said that?"

"Why, I heard him—"

"Mr. Doone!" called some authoritative person.

They had blindfolded Clancy after a mighty struggle and stripped him of saddle and bridle once more. Now the corral was cleared of all saving the stallion, sweat-blackened, with a bright glimmer of blood red shining through here and there— a beautiful and sinister figure. His victory made him tower

54

greater than his actual size. He had become a monster. Two of the cow ponies rolled together would not make his match. And he walked about, conscious of his strength, flattening his ears wickedly as he neared the fence, reveling in the hatred and the awe and the covetousness which showed in the eyes of the humans and their voices as he came by.

"Mr. Doone!" called that commanding voice again.

Holden identified the speaker, a big-shouldered man past middle age, but very vigorous still, to judge by the spring in his walk—a square-jawed, handsome man. One might almost have said that he looked too much the fighter and the conqueror to really be one. Toward him approached a lank old cattleman in a faded blue flannel shirt, his vest unbuttoned, the tag of his tobacco sack dangling in the wind. Holden noticed every detail of his dress.

"All right, Mr. Larramee," said the cowman.

Holden forgot himself; and then remembered himself with a shudder and a wave of cold. This was the father of Alexa. Somehow the fact that a millionaire chose to dress himself so roughly, so like any other rancher, made Holden dread him and his wrath all the more.

The two had drawn together. Under the tree the doctor was busy over Al Morton, and a sobbing woman sat by Al's head. But though half a dozen watched this group, the majority chose to follow the movements of Larramee and Doone.

"Now look here, Doone," said the great man, "this ought to be proof positive that no one can handle that brute of a horse."

"I dunno," said Doone. "They's still another month. On the third is my boy's birthday. *He'd* of rode that hoss, I figger. Well, we got till then for somebody to ride Clancy."

"No one except a madman will ever try to handle that killer," said Larramee. "You know that, Doone."

"I'm not askin' no one. I say, they's still a month, about."

"And what then?"

"A slug of lead for Clancy. I guess that's all for him!"

Mr. Larramee had grown greatly excited. So had the crowd, and its eagerness to hear allowed Holden to make out every word with great exactness.

"You don't mean it, Doone. You really don't mean that you'd throw away a magnificent life such as this?"

"What's a hoss made for?" asked Doone.

"Why, to be used, of course."

"No," said Doone, "to be mastered. That's what it's made for. I'd *give* the hoss to him that could ride him. I wouldn't sell him for a million."

"Come, come!" said Larramee. "We'll talk about this together when you——"

"It ain't no use, sir. I'd like to please you, but I can't. I think about my boy. He was like this hoss. Nobody never mastered him. He raised the devil all his life. Maybe it was a pretty good thing for the world when he died. All because I didn't teach him nothin'. Well, the same way with this hoss. I ain't gunna turn him out to kill folks. And that's what he'll do."

"I'll manage to handle him. And he'll be immensely valuable to me. That blood and that bone—he'll change the blood of my saddle stock and give me the finest set of range horses in the mountains. I need that Clancy. I have to have him, Doone, and I tell you frankly that I don't give up my ambitions easily."

At this, Doone thrust out his jaw. "Money is one thing," said he. "And you got lots of it. But ideas is something, too. And this here idea of mine you can't buy, no matter how hard or how high you go after it. I don't let Clancy go except to a gent that can handle him!"

Larramee struck a fist against his open palm, then changed his mind.

"That's final?" he snapped out.

"Mr. Larramee, I'm dog-gone sorry. That's final, sir!"

11

It occurred to Holden that he was wasting a golden opportunity here. The entire town was gathered here to see the place where the gladiators had striven together. Now was his opportunity, if ever, to slip away unobserved.

He paused only to dash some water over his face, untie the chain of Sneak, and fix his hat on his head, but as he turned to the door, a knock came upon it, and when he answered in a voice in which there was a groan, that door was opened by the strong hand of Mr. Oliphant Larramee himself—the great Larramee of Aunt Carrie's narrative—the father of beautiful Alexa.

At the very first glimpse of the strongly squared jaw of this hero, poor little Tom Holden's strength melted from his soul and melted from his limbs. He slipped into a chair simply because he had not strength enough to remain standing. And as the big rancher closed the door behind him, Holden felt the keen glance of the man of money go over him, little by little, missing nothing—not even the fact that he was not cleanly shaven for this morning.

Little—weak—unclean! Such must be the conclusions in the mind of Mr. Larramee. When shame reaches a certain point, it can go no farther. It begins to destroy itself. There was too much shame in Holden to pass into solution. The excess of that emotion of his soul served him as a false power and sustained him.

"I have been expecting you," said Holden. "Won't you sit down?"

Larramee drew off his gloves without answering, still eyeing his host. He said at length: "I presume we know one another; this is Mr. Holden?"

"This is. And you are Mr. Larramee."

"I am."

He dropped the gloves into a pocket; then he dropped his hands upon his hips. Holden thought that he had never confronted a more alert figure, no matter what the age of the other. There could be no doubt what the removal of those gloves meant. Mr. Larramee presumed that this conversation might lead to physical violence—or to gun play! And his readiness for either termination was thus implied.

"In the meantime," said he, "you seem to know my daughter also, Mr. Holden."

Holden shrugged his shoulders.

"You even seem to know her," said the rancher, "a little better than she knows you."

"I have no doubt," said Holden.

"Ah," said Larramee, flushing. "You have no doubt?"

"None whatever."

Mr. Larramee drew in a breath. It was plain that he was taking a gigantic grip upon a gigantic temper.

"Won't you sit down?" asked Holden.

"I shall not sit down," said Mr. Larramee with much terseness.

Holden could not tell whether this display of irritability did more to frighten him or to give him an odd reassurance.

"I believe in looking into every phase of all the matters that enter my life—when there is time," said Larramee. "I have looked into you, sir. I have been to the house of Miss Davis—"

"Who is she, sir?"

"Do you mean to tell me that you deny having been in her house last night?"

"Ah," said Holden. "She is the witch?"

Mr. Larramee blinked at him.

"You seem to be extraordinarily fond of riddles," said he. "Well, let that be as it is. What I have to say to you, young man, has to do with a matter which most definitely concerns me. My daughter—" He paused, as though feeling that he had begun in an awkward manner.

"Miss Larramee is charming," said Holden soothingly.

At this, Larramee started and stamped. "Your commendation," said he, "is—very kind. In the meantime, it appears that you do more than commend her?"

"I do."

"You even announce that you are to be married to her?"

"I believe that I have made a remark of that nature."

Mr. Larramee turned a dark, dark red. "By the eternal heavens," said he, "I am a patient man, sir. I believe that I am a just man. But on this one subject I thank God that I am as touchy as a young colt. What was in your mind, Mr. Holden, when you presumed to make such a remark about a girl—"

"Who has never seen me?"

"Exactly."

"First of all—may I ask you what Miss Davis had to say about me?"

"It was extraordinary. If it were not for what she had to say, I tell you frankly, Mr. Holden, I should have had you tarred and feathered and ridden on a rail out of this town! But it appears that she found you—extraordinary, to say the least."

"As for the tar and feathers," said Holden coldly, "I

presume that you know to whom you are speaking? Or did Miss Davis make that point clear?"

He waited. There was not a chance in ten that she had not betrayed that he was a harmless weakling who had won a great conquest by a great bluff.

"She told me," said Larramee, "that your actions spoke for themselves. As for the quelling of that town nuisance, the bully Crogan—it was a confounded commendable thing. I grant that. As for what else you are other than a gun fighter and adventurer—I wait for the information with much curiosity. But as for the remark through which you connected yourself with my daughter—why, darn me, Mr. Holden, such a—" He paused, not quite ready to commit himself to a denunciation.

"You would say that every man has a right to speak what is his expectation?" asked Holden.

"Naturally. But in heaven's name, my dear young man, unless you are mad—"

"I only spoke," said Holden, "what I hope to make true."

Mr. Larramee reached for the wall and supported himself against it. "Go on," said he. "I am a very patient man. Explain yourself."

"I had to bring my hope to your attention. You perhaps will wonder why I did not come to you in person to—"

"Not at all," said Larramee grimly. "I might have been overcome by a desire to throw you out of the house by the nape of the neck."

"Certainly," said Holden gravely. "That was in my mind. And if you had done such a thing I should have been in a quandary. Of course I would have been physically too weak to resist you. I should have been forced to submit, and thereby be shamed forever in your eyes and in the eyes of Miss Larramee. Or else, I should have been compelled to kill you, Mr. Larramee."

The great man grunted.

"It was so difficult for me to decide," said Holden, making a graceful gesture, "that I thought it would be best to use general rumor."

Mr. Larramee sat down suddenly and with jarring weight. "Young Mr. Holden," said he, "I begin to agree with Miss Davis that you are an extraordinary youth. Somewhere hidden behind all of this there is an immense jest, I have no doubt. You are an intelligent fellow. You seem to be well educated. You have the command of your brains. For these reasons I am still in this room waiting for you to explain yourself."

Holden trailed his fingers through the shaggy scalp of Sneak. Then he looked up.

"I shall tell you the exact truth, I saw the picture of your daughter and fell in love with it. I heard she was to be at the dance and went there to see her. As I looked at her, some one spoke to me. And I uttered my thoughts aloud. That, sir, is the entire story."

The rapid glance of the big man measured him again. "This is apparently a serious truth," said he, almost gently.

"Entirely."

"You propose yourself as a suitor for the hand of my daughter Alexa?"

"I do."

"And your grounds for hope?"

"Are my love for her, sir, and the hope that I may prove worthy of her."

A dazed expression passed across the eyes of Mr. Larramee. He looked rather wildly about him, found no help, and uttered a long sigh.

"I am a very bewildered man," said he.

"What qualifications must a man have?" asked Holden. "Money?"

"Money be darned!" said the millionaire. He rose from his chair and walked to the window. "The entire countryside is talking about this," he said to himself rather than to his host. "Poor Alexa!"

The cripple raised himself from the chair and hobbled to the window also. "Tell me," said he, "what can I do to make my peace? With you, Mr. Larramee, and perhaps with her also."

Mr. Larramee looked down upon him. Then he glanced hastily out the window.

"Do you see that horse?" said he.

"Clancy? Yes."

"Ride that horse to my ranch house."

Holden sighed. "And then?" said he.

"And then we may consider ourselves introduced."

"And Miss Larramee?"

60

The rich man stamped. "What of her?" he asked impatiently.

Holden grew pale. "Will you yourself introduce me to her?"

"What!"

"If I ride out the horse to your ranch—"

"In that case," said Larramee, with a faint smile, "I shall be very happy to introduce you to her. In the meantime, her name—"

"I shall never mention her again, without your permission."

12

AFTER THE HEAVY stride of Larramee went down the corridor and then thudded along the stairs and disappeared, it was a long time before Holden gathered the shattered bits of his self-control and was able to take Sneak on the chain and lead him downstairs. He met the proprietor in the little lobby. It was the last person in the world he would have chosen to encounter, but the proprietor did not laugh. He did not even smile.

"Been talkin' to Mr. Larramee?" he asked pleasantly.

And Holden, bewildered, was aware that the rich man had not spoken his mind in public. For that, he blessed his fortunate stars.

"We had quite a chat," said he easily. "Is it too late to get some breakfast?"

"Not for a friend of Mr. Larramee's!" said the host, and in person he escorted his guest into the dining room, and in person he braved the impatient anger of the Chinese cook which was audible behind the swinging door, and in person, moreover, he sat down at Holden's table and held him in talk.

But to the questions of where he first knew Mr. Larramee and when that meeting took place, Holden replied with vague responses. Such a great impression had been made upon the excellent proprietor by the visit from the great Larramee, however, that after breakfast he insisted upon moving the room of Holden to the best chamber in the hotel, which was not good enough to be worth remark, at that! In the meantime, through the window, Holden kept watch upon the little white house of Aunt Carrie in the distance, and presently, as he had expected, he saw the form of Mr. Larramee issue from it in haste, slam the gate open, sweep onto the back of a horse, and spur furiously away before the gate had time to swing shut. After that Holden left his host to his own devices and hurried forth to the house of the witch with the great dog at his heels.

He found Aunt Carrie muttering to herself in the garden and stabbing viciously at the soil with a trowel. When his shadow fell across her, she wrenched out a handful of weeds without looking up.

"Well," said the witch, "you have brought me the first call I've received from Mr. Larramee since I left his house. Two calls from him, in fact!" She looked up at him. "And a pretty state of mind you left him in," she went on. "He doesn't know whether you're completely mad or simply foolish. He doesn't know whether to have you mobbed or bribe you to stay away."

"We had quite a talk," admitted Holden.

"That dog still has a hollow look," said Aunt Carrie dubiously. "Has it had breakfast?"

"Yes."

"After all," said she, "I swore that he'd have to be the first one to come. I swore that I'd never cross his threshold before he asked my pardon for certain things he said."

"I'm glad that I brought you some good," said Holden.

"You?" she cried. "Well, of all things! You're the picture of complacence, I must say, young Mr. Holden!"

Young Mr. Holden sat down on an inverted flowerpot and prodded the soil with the end of his staff. "He is to introduce me himself," said he dreamily.

Aunt Carrie leaped to her feet. "What?" cried she.

"He's to introduce me himself," repeated he sleepily. "What did you tell him about me?"

"Nothing!" she answered. "But—what lies have you been telling that man about yourself?"

"Not very many. This was a bargain."

"Come, come," said the lady. "I know the faults of Oliphant Larramee, but to bargain about his daughter was never among his bad qualities. He'd as soon deal lightly with heaven, if he believed in anything. Alexa is the nearest thought to heaven that he has!"

"I am to be introduced," said he, "when I ride Clancy out to the Larramee house."

"Sacred heaven!" cried Miss Carrie Davis. "You don't mean that you'll attempt it, child?"

"For her?" asked Holden.

Miss Davis seized upon him and led him into the house. "You *are* mad," said she, when she had planted him in a chair so violently that Sneak favored her with a terrible snarl. "Clancy would eat you like a buttered biscuit."

"I am going to let him try," said Holden, making a wry face.

She folded her skinny arms and shook her head. "There *is* a devil in you, then," said she. "I told Larramee that much. That was when he started laughing at you."

"Did he laugh, then?"

"Not long. I straightened him out. Now, Tom Holden, you've made my girl the common talk of the town, and what are you going to do about it?"

"I don't know," said he. "I won't know until I see her. Can you manage that?"

"Get out!" snapped out Aunt Carrie. "You have almost ruined her good name already. If you dare to mention her again as long as you live, I'll tell the whole world that you're a bluff and a sham!" She escorted him to the door.

There he paused. "The whole world," said he, "might not believe you."

He was more comfortable, when he went back to the hotel. That day he spent most of his time at the window looking down at the great stallion, until big Clancy came to know that he was there. Sometimes, when the monster was strolling about the enclosure, he would whirl suddenly about and shake his head at Holden. Once he actually snorted and stamped and flattened his ears at the sight of the impassive face in the window. But Holden paid no heed. He was growing used to the horse from a distance. In the meantime, he was turning over many thoughts in his mind. He had enough money to live on for a time. That money which Chris Venner had forced on him still was not exhausted. If so small a portion of it had amounted to two hundred dollars, what must the entire sum have been?

He ate a late supper after the other guests were finished, and then he went out to the corral. He had a folding chair and a small bundle of hay, all with the wheat heads attached. And he sat down at a far corner of the corral and took a handful of the hay and extended it between the bars. There was a pair of tall shrubs which sheltered him from view upon either side. No one missed the broken old chair from the veranda. He was all alone with his work, which consisted in simply sitting there hour after hour with some of the wheat heads protruding through the bars of the corral.

At first it was nervous work. Sometimes big Clancy leaped at him and tried to wedge his snaky head and neck through the bars to get at him with his teeth. Sometimes he raced off around the enclosure, tossing up his heels and his head and snorting. Sometimes he sneaked up on the place little by little and made a sudden dart at the end. And at other times he pretended to be totally oblivious of the presence of the man— a pretense which he kept up for hours. But if he wanted to drink, Clancy had to come to the trough, and the trough was fairly under the hand of the stranger. And if he did not drink, the heat of the night air, and the thirst which nervousness brought on him, was a torment. And when he came to drink, there were the tempting wheat heads, with the terrible human scent behind them. Clancy was fairly sweating with fear and anger before an hour had passed. And if the smell of the sweet wheat heads did not draw him, the need of water did!

In the meantime, with growing patience, Holden watched the dimly glimmering form of the horse by the starlight, and he watched the dark shapes of the evergreens which stood in the copse near by, and he listened to the voices of the town. They were very many. At first there was chiefly the racket of children playing through the streets of Larramee. Afterward these noises and the sounds of the tins rattling in the dish waters of many kitchens, passed away, and there followed pairs of voices passing up and down. Usually there were men talking with women. Sometimes woman and woman; sometimes man and man went by, murmuring. He heard little snatches of talk, for who could have guessed that an eaves-dropper was crouched there in the sparse brush, so close to the corral of terrible Clancy?

Once two men came and leaned on the corral fence.

"Three weeks for Clancy, and then a gun!" said one. "That's a devil of an end for a hoss like him!"

"Where do devils belong?" asked the other.

And then he heard two girls chattering. Their voices were not loud, but they were pitched so high that he could hear the penetrating sounds long before they reached him and long after they went by.

"*Will* he marry her?"

"I hope not!"

"It would be a wonder, I guess."

"Sort of horrible, I think."

"But he said that he would."

"Maybe he was lying."

"Well, would a man dare to lie about a girl like that?"

"I don't know. He's not like other men."

"And she's so beautiful."

"She ain't so very much. I seen Minne Slawson last month in Tuckhony. She looked a pile prettier than Alexa Larramee ever did."

"Well, she's too pretty to waste on a cripple, anyway."

They were talking of him—and of the girl! Even to have the thing talked about made it more possible, somehow. He listened, half tortured, half enraptured.

"Her father will never—"

"You can't tell. You know he came in and talked a long time with Holden today."

"You don't mean it!"

"He did, though."

"Maybe this Holden knows something about Mr. Larramee."

"Maybe! Besides, he's queer."

"Of course. They say he's made that wolf as tame as a dog. He just has to give it a look. The wolf understands."

"Is it really a wolf?"

"Dad heard Harry describe it. He says that it's sure a wolf. A real lobo!"

"I don't see how he dares!"

"He dared big Crogan."

"I saw Louise Crogan this morning. She says—"

What Louise had to say was lost on Holden. The voices at this point finally faded out down the street and only broken fragments came back to him as he listened, but it was enough to convince him that the mind of the town was still full of him. He went back to his room in the morning with the first gray of the dawn, for no one must note the manner in which he spent his time with big Clancy. After all, it promised to be a long hunt, for Clancy had not yet so much as torn at the wheat heads!

He slept then, until noon. All the afternoon he drowsed at the window of his room, keeping a dim lookout toward the little white house with the red roof and the green blinds. And it was almost evening, it was the very golden hour of the late day, when he saw her canter a graceful stepping bay up to the hitching rack in front of Aunt Carrie's house.

He knew that it was she. He knew it by the carriage of her head and by something in the modeling of her shoulders and the nape of her neck—something more delicately finished than in other women. Then, as she dismounted, the sun struck her face, and he saw her smile and wave to Aunt Carrie, who was coming through the door of the little house and running to greet her guest.

Holden looked again, then reached excitedly for his hat and staff and hurried from his room.

13

IT DID NOT occur to him to think of the morality of the thing. He was embarked in a desperate venture in which he must use every weapon on which he could lay his hands. If he could help himself by merely using his ears, certainly he would do so. He had already picked out a path. It led from the back of the hotel to the back of Miss Davis' house, and by keeping to the shelter between a long arbor and a hedge, he was able to come well up to the house itself and then crouch beneath a window.

The sound of their voices guided him. He circled the house with cautious haste; finally crouched beneath a window of the living room, he could hear everything plainly. It was mostly the voice of Alexa, and he listened to it with his eyes shut. It was an inner light, showing him her face, and her soul. For what are the eyes and what do they take in, compared with the delicate nuances which the ear perceives and knows in every finest shade of meaning at once? She was telling of a visit—of a letter from an old friend—of a new horse which her father had given her—of a trip planned for Spain the next spring, but the eavesdropper paid no heed to all of this. A pause came in the current of her talking.

"Does your father know that you've come to see me?"

"I won't have to hide that any more. Not since *he* came to see you himself."

"What did he say?"

"I think, Aunt Carrie, that he's afraid of you."

"Tush! Oliphant Larramee?"

"That very man. He really is. He would have smashed that insolent rascal to bits, if you hadn't spoken in favor of the— oh, Aunt Carrie, why did you do that? You were just being perverse. Confess it!"

"If I had given him a bad report, what would your father have done?"

"I hardly dare to think!"

"Neither did I. So I gave him a rather good report. I didn't want your father hanged for murder, you know. Not so much for his sake as for yours."

"Aunt Carrie!"

"That was only part of it. Chiefly, I was afraid for him. I wouldn't let him go storming at such a tiger as that Tom Holden!"

"But he's only a cripple!"

"He was enough to manage Crogan."

"Crogan is a stupid bully. This Holden simply outwitted him; his smartness and not his courage beat Crogan."

"Let me tell you, Alexa, I was here in this room, and listened. Crogan came here to kill if ever I saw a man ready for a killing. And I could watch him change his mind. It was a dreadful thing to see his manhood wither away in front of that terrible boy!"

"Is he so young?"

"In his early twenties."

"How queer!"

"Without his glasses, extraordinarily good looking."

"Why should such a desperate man have had——"

"Eyes? Study spoiled them, I suppose. Quite a student. Bookish, you know. You can always tell the touch!"

"Exactly! But Aunt Carrie—what's he doing, rioting in a town like this? Playing bad man on the range?"

"Tush, dear. What has he done? He saved the life of a dog that a lot of brutal boys were murdering. Then he came into my house and talked to me. Then he outfaced Crogan. And he——"

"And afterwards dared to say—oh, if word of this ever gets to my Eastern friends, I'll never hear the end of it. Do you know that he actually said that he intended to marry me?"

"I suppose he does."

"Aunt Carrie!"

"Do you blame a man for wanting to marry a girl like you?"

"But he implied—I've spent the whole day denying it. And it does no good. The harder I talk the more people smile and look knowing."

"You had best stop talking and begin praying, my dear, if you want to keep yourself out of the hands of that fellow."

"Aunt Carrie, what on earth do you mean?"

"He's the sort of a man that has his own way in the end."

"I had rather——" she began strongly, but the older woman interrupted.

"I know. I've heard girls say that before. But it makes no difference. It isn't what you want to do. It's what your nature forces you to do against your will. That's what counts between a man and a woman. And this Holden, he's the most difficult sort to understand."

"Why?"

"Because he's much stronger than he thinks he is. He really thinks that he's a simple fellow. As a matter of fact—he staggered me, Alexa, as much as he outfaced Crogan."

"I should think he would stagger any one, with his impertinence! However, I imagine that we'll soon learn something. Father is having him watched. Do you know that he was away from the hotel all of last night?"

"Really?"

"No one knows where. But still we're watching. Dad will find out. Of course the man is up to some villainy. I—I hope that they land him in jail."

"Because he loves you, Alexa?"

"Aunt Carrie! How can you use such a word to dignify—the—the—"

"What?"

"I don't know," sighed Alexa. "These men are too difficult to understand. But—but—"

"Open the window," said Aunt Carrie. "Open it a little wider than it is—it's too warm in here. No, I'll do it myself."

Tom Holden heard her steps approaching and strove to slip away through the flowers, but just as he started, he caught his toe between two stones and jammed his shoe. He had to pause to disentangle it, and looking up in a horror of guilty fright, he found Aunt Carrie looking coldly, emotionlessly down to him, nodding slowly in agreement with some former conviction.

As for Holden, having disentangled himself, he waited in a frenzy of cold fear. If the girl should ever hear that he was a common eavesdropper, that would be the end of him. Then he heard Aunt Carrie say: "We've talked enough about that man Holden."

"But, Aunt Carrie, that's just what I wanted—"

"Nonsense. He isn't so much bother. A little runt of an insignificant cripple!" She raised her harsh voice until it rang: "A little poverty-stricken nobody! Bah!"

"But you just said that he—"

"Nonsense! Every woman has a divine right to change her mind and tell the truth. Now—"

Holden was gone. Those last whiplash sentences had seared his very soul and left scars which would not soon disappear. He crept back to the hotel by the back way. And in his room he fell on his bed and lay with his arms cast out wide, staring at the ceiling, wondering why he chose to keep his wretched life on this painful earth.

For he was all of that—a poverty-stricken little nobody—not worth conversation on his behalf. What further truths would Aunt Carrie be prompted to speak concerning him? Then a new thought made him sit up suddenly. For it occurred to him that if she had intended to ruin him with Alexa forever, she would simply have lowered her voice and told the girl what she had just seen. Instead, she had preferred to speak so that Holden himself could not fail to understand what she said. Perhaps she was punishing him, but reserving a greater mercy.

The dark came, and he went out to his odd task again. There was a difference in the stallion at once. Perhaps his rations had not been overgenerous that day, but at any rate, he came to the wheat heads at once and ripped them out of the fingers of Holden and flaunted across the corral with them, snorting with triumph. There he waited until he had devoured them. But there was still the fragrance of the wheat heads to draw him back. He came again and again he stole. He came still again, and this time, his twitching, prehensile upper lip touched the fingers of the man's hand and Clancy leaped backward and whirled away with a shudder of hatred and fear.

All of this was before the waiting of Holden had lasted an hour. And by midnight, Clancy was eating crumbled wheat heads out of the naked palm of Holden!

That was midnight, and long before dawn Holden sat inside the bars of the corral, waiting, waiting, the wheat heads in his hand.

Once big Clancy dashed at him and reared to beat his skull to bits with a few hammer strokes of his forehoofs. But the stallion dropped down without having struck. Once Clancy wheeled and lashed out with heels that went whirring six inches over the head of the seated form. But something told Holden that this miss was carefully calculated beforehand. And just before the gray of the dawn began, Clancy came to him and smelled him and sniffed him from head to heel, and pushed off his hat with mischievous muzzle, and nibbled at his hair, and pinched the flesh of his shoulder cruelly with his teeth, and then, pawing, struck the shins of Holden with a brutally heavy hoof.

There was this one reward, that Holden, raising a slow and cautious hand, was able to touch the sleek muzzle of the stallion and thereby bestow upon it the first caress of its life!

When that was done, he felt that he had conquered half a kingdom! He slipped out of the corral and went back to the hotel and so up to his room.

Just as he opened the door, a shadow slipped out upon either side of him and grasped his skinny arms. Steel glinted in the shadows of the dawn; and rasping voices jarred in his ear.

"He'll have it on him," said one. "Give him a look-over now!"

With that, in silence, he was handcuffed. And in the grip of these giants he knew that the first effort to struggle or to escape by force would be to expose his terrible, his incredible weakness. So he stood quietly. They searched him from head to foot. Finally, when they had probed his boots and turned out every pocket, they stood back, gloomy and silent.

"One of you," said Holden, "is the sheriff, I suppose?"

"Where was you last night?" asked a gruff voice.

Holden swelled his chest and made his voice loud. "Whistling at the moon," said he. "Where were you?"

"He must of buried it, sheriff," muttered the second man.

"Talk up," said the sheriff, "and tell us what and who was with you, and who tipped you off and fixed the plant, and I'll see what can be done for you, Holden. I mean, you tell me that, knowin' that you're under arrest right now!"

"Thanks," said Holden. "I am going to write down the names of both of you men and never forget them. In the meantime, I'll be glad to tell you what I was doing. I was taking a walk through the trees—"

The sheriff's companion snarled like an angry dog, but the sheriff himself merely shrugged his shoulders in the lamplight.

"It's no use," said he. "This gent is too smart. He put the stuff away before he come back, and now we got nothin' on him. Holden, you're loose."

14

THERE IN THE darkness followed a hurried consultation.

"Ain't you gunna do nothin'?" asked the sheriff's assistant. "Are you gunna let him go free, to raise hell with us when he catches us one by one, later on?"

"The law is the law," declared the sheriff, "which we ain't got nothin' agin' this gent. He says that he was walkin' around all night amusin' himself. Which we ain't got no proof that he wasn't. And we got to do the provin'! Holden," he continued, "all I'm sayin' to you is that we're watchin' you all the time and we're watchin' you close. If you so much as look crooked, we'll have you mighty pronto!"

With this warning, spoken in a very unforceful fashion, the men of the law departed from the room and left Holden to his reflections. But whatever they were, he was too exhausted by his night watch to ponder anything very long. In ten minutes he was sound asleep, and he did not stir in his place in the bed until three in the afternoon.

Then he sat up, with his head hot and ringing, and his eyes dull, and the face which looked back at him from the bit of mirror over the chest of drawers was worn and pale. How could these strong men of the cattle ranges, these fierce and willing fighters, look upon him for an instant without realizing that he was a mere shell of weakness?

But when he came down the stairs, he was received with a solemn gloom on the brow of the proprietor. He was led into the dining room at once as a privileged guest.

"Late hours is hard on the eyes," observed the host sullenly, staring down at the worn eyes of the little man, but Holden, overcome with feeble languor, had not even energy enough to enable him to smile back at the other. He looked sadly down to the floor, and stroked the savage head of Sneak.

After that late breakfast, he went on down the street to the white house of the witch and knocked at her door. He knew by a stir and then a whispering silence in the place that she was there and that she had heard him, but she did not answer. He did not knock again. He merely waited in silence, leaning on his staff, his hat in his hand.

Five, ten, perhaps fifteen minutes he waited there, growing faint with the effort. Then the door was snatched open and Miss Davis stood before him, glowering.

"Why d'you come sneaking up to me?" said she. "I don't want to see you ever again."

"Of course not," murmured Holden, not daring to meet her angry eyes.

"Then why are you here? What are you doing, moping around my front door?"

"The longer you punished me out here," said he with the most abject submission, "the less I thought you'd punish me afterward."

"Punish you? Bah!" cried the witch. "What have I to do

with a fellow who comes sneaking and crawling—to listen to ladies talking together?"

"I have nothing to say," admitted he miserably, "except that I'm playing a lone hand against great odds, Aunt Carrie —Miss Davis, I mean!"

"At least," she said sneeringly, "you are not trying to live up to your foolish contract with big Clancy. You are wise enough not to risk your neck with that devil, any of these days, no matter what you do for a living, wandering around at night, Mr. Hold-up Man Holden!"

She shrugged her shoulders. "The whole town knows all about you," she said cruelly. "It knows about the robberies that are going on. It knows that you sneak out of the hotel at night. And when they catch you red-handed—there'll be a lynching, Mr. Holden. I promise you that! The patience of this town of Larramee won't last forever!"

He turned this matter hastily in his mind. Since he was perfectly guiltless of any such intention as robbery, and since the suspicion against him helped to bolster up the idea that he was a formidable character, it was as well, he thought, to allow them to continue in the error of their ways. Moreover, while they looked for him abroad, committing outrages here and there about the countryside, it would all the better shield him in his work with the stallion in the corral at night.

"You will never forgive me, then," he asked Aunt Carrie sadly.

"What difference does it make, whether I forgive you or not?" she snapped out at him. "Will my forgiveness help to make you a better man?"

"Immensely better," he vowed to her. "And—did you tell her—"

"Don't mention her name!" cried the tyrannical witch. "You are not worthy to mention her name. I'll not hear you do it, on my honor!"

"I hope to do as you wish," said he faintly.

"Then leave Larramee!"

"Do you mean that?"

"Of course I do!"

"After all," he said, "if I have not your assistance and good advice, I might as well surrender at once and leave the town, I suppose. Good-by, Miss Davis," and he started away.

"Come back here," she commanded.

He turned slowly toward her.

"You are a rascal," said Aunt Carrie. "But I really think that you've been punished enough. No, I didn't tell Alexa. If she hasn't wit enough to find out what sort of a man you are, and find it out to her own satisfaction—"

"If I ever meet her," sighed he.

"Do you depend upon *me* for that introduction?"

"Of course not. I depend on Clancy, you know."

"Heavens, child! Do you really intend to try your hand with that brute?"

"I am reading about horse training," said the liar smoothly. "And when I know a little more, I'll start in."

"You've never handled horses at all?" she asked.

"Never. It would be hard for me to sit in a saddle, you know, unless I were tied in."

Aunt Carrie threw up a hand in dismay. "Well," said she, "you *are* a madman. Now go back and get some sleep. You are worn out—with your raids and your rantings around the country at night! The next time you try it, my fine young man, you'll get a bullet through your head. That will be sauce for your pudding, I presume!"

He left the little white house immensely relieved, and going to the edge of the town, he sat for a long time under the shade of a tree watching Sneak made frantic and foolish efforts to catch little fish which were drifting over the bright, sun-yellowed shoal water of a pool at his feet. Holden closed his eyes and dreamed, and felt the strength from the soil pass up into his exhausted body and felt the peace and the deep surety of the woods enter into his mind.

After that, in the dusk, he went back to the hotel. It was a lonely time of the day, when houseless men listened with empty hearts to the cheerful voices of other men, and when the calling and the crying of children has an added meaning. To these things Holden listened, and then he turned his head to the north and looked up to the great house on the distant hill, already blackening against the sunset colors which ringed the horizon.

He idled through the early evening; but the full darkness had barely closed down on the town before he was again in the corral with Clancy. He was greeted even as on the night before with a charge and a rearing of that gigantic body above him, but the stallion dropped down again, quietly, to all fours. He began to sniff Holden from head to foot; knocked off the hat of the patient cripple; nibbled again at his hair; and so submitted at last, to have his muzzle rubbed while he ate the wheat heads.

Then Holden rose and stood by the monster. As he rose, little by little, Clancy shrank away to the farther side of the corral. There he stood shaking his fine head until the mane flowed and bristled in the air like a stiffened crest. But there was still the same fragrance of wheat heads, and the low, murmuring voice of this man was unlike other human voices. Other humans yelled, and their words were like little explosions. Other men snarled and whined and shrilled like beasts —like dogs and hateful wolves, for instance. But this man was different. There was another thing in his voice than a mere noise. There was something to listen to, something almost to be understood; something which remained, ever, just around the corner from intelligibility.

So Clancy began to come back to the man, little by little, stopping to paw the earth like an angered bull, and then snort and shake his head, as though denouncing himself because he trusted one of these dangerous humans for even the split part of a second!

It was only the third night. But when once the door of the confidence of a horse has been opened, be it no more than a glimpse of light, there is apt to be a rapid progress toward an understanding. But before that third night was over, Holden was able to stand at the head of the stallion and put an arm around his neck!

It was very exhausting work, almost like handling fire, hour after hour, and when the dawn came again, Holden was half dead with exhaustion in his bed. He slept like a drugged man until the late afternoon. Then he rose, ate as before, solitary in the dining room, and waited for the coming of the night.

That was his program for day after day and for night after night. In the meantime, the depredations of the outlaw who was raiding the country during this same period became, night by night, more terrible. He was a small man—a man about the build of Tom Holden. And he was a merciless killer, who preferred to leave his victims dead behind him, rather than to let them live to give testimony against him, perhaps, at a later date.

And, during this time, as Holden slipped out of the hotel

night after night, on every evening the sheriff or one of his men entered the dark room of Holden after his departure, and searched it carefully, methodically, regardless of the vicious snarling of Sneak, where he was tied at the foot of the bed. But they found nothing—not a sign of a clew which could lead them into the past crimes of this suspected man or point toward any of his future plans. It seemed, however, a most dreadful thing that the great Larramee should actually entertain the thought of this criminal as a son-in-law to be!

The sheriff in person called on Larramee and stated all of his suspicions frankly and freely. When he was ended, Mr. Larramee responded with no heat whatever.

"My dear sir," said he, "I do not criticize the actions of this remarkable young man. I have never said that he is to be the future husband of my daughter. I have never said that he was *not* to be. On the contrary, I want him to work out his own way. I only hope that I shall not be a stumbling block in his path. You say he is a robber. It may be that he is. Then, my dear sir, I entreat you to find him in a crime and put him in prison. Certainly I do not wish to have my daughter married to a thug and an outlaw! But—how does the rascal manage to ride a horse, considering that withered leg of his?"

15

THIS REMARK, which could not be considered by the sheriff as other than extremely inopportune, caused him to ride most thoughtfully back to the town, but he had no sooner reached the village of Larramee than he was encountered by news which was so exactly in the same vein with his own thoughts and the recent suggestion of the rich man, that he was filled with amazement and could hardly believe his ears. Neither, for that matter, could the rest of Larramee.

For the astonishing tidings were as follows: Mr. Doone, the owner of the terrible Clancy, had been formally challenged that evening to submit his horse to the test the next day and live up to his promise to give the stallion away to any man who could ride it. This was exciting enough. But the excitement was trebled by the fact that he who had challenged was none other than, of all the men in the world, the mysterious and terrible cripple, Tom Holden!

The first general comment was that of the rich rancher. They had not thought of it before, while Holden was being accused of careering abroad from one end of the country to the other, robbing here, murdering there with a red-handed abandon. But when they considered the problem of such a cripple mastering the great Clancy, they were aghast. How could he sit the saddle with that withered leg?

Mr. Doone held a consultation of his friends. "Him that can ride Clancy fair and square," said he, "gets that hoss, and heaven knows I'm proud to see the gent that can do it. But it ain't in Tom Holden to be that man. No, sir. If he aims to ride my Clancy, then it means that he's got some manner of trick up his sleeve."

This idea was considered highly sensible. The next thing was to arrive at what sort of trick might be available to a man who wanted to ride a dangerous horse.

"Dope!" said some one. "He'll dope Clancy and make him so dog-gone down-headed that any kid could manage him."

This suggestion was considered highly probable. Indeed, it was hardly suggested before it was taken for granted that this must be the plan of the mysterious cripple, and muttering curses to one another and promising Mr. Holden eternal bad luck for his wickedness, a guard of half a dozen men volunteered to stand guard over the corral of the stallion that night and see that he was kept untampered with for the morning of the trial. Others hurried away to inform their friends in the countryside that the great duel between Clancy and mankind was about to see the writing of another chapter and the fighting of another bout. And the contestant was to be Tom Holden himself, the robber, the gun fighter, the man of mystery.

Wickedness is always attractive. It was doubly attractive to have two very wicked characters opposed to one another. Here was a villain among horses staked against a villain among men, and the town of Larramee and all of the surrounding countryside told itself that it would not miss the contest. Word even came out to Mr. Larramee, and he could not avoid the test. He started in for town, and his daughter

77

rode beside him. And every road to Larramee was thick with hurrying travelers, all fearful that they might miss a single vital chapter in this strange tale.

When poor Tom Holden sat down at the window of his room that morning and looked down upon the throng, he found that a full thousand men and women and children were already gathered there about the corral in spite of the early hour. Twice the crowd that had come to watch even such a famous buckaroo as Al Morton. And, on the outskirts of the crowd, sitting in a buggy with a fine span hitched in the traces, he saw the square shoulders and the handsome face of Mr. Larramee himself, with Alexa at his side.

A sort of sad courage poured into the body of Holden, at that, and into his heart. He went down at once, and when he appeared, there was a general muttering of hatred and of astonishment—astonishment that he was actually coming to make the trial of himself against the horse! And how small he seemed, and how infinitely mighty seemed the stallion!

Another thing that boded ill for poor Tom Holden—the stallion all that night had showed himself strangely ill at ease. He had paced up and down and up and down the corral, sometimes striding toward one of the watchers as far as the fence would permit, and sometimes toward another, but always shaking his head and snorting his anger and disappointment.

At first they thought that he was merely trying to get out at them. Then they decided that the great animal was actually looking for something which it missed. What could that be? At least all were agreed that Clancy was wildly excited long before the morning came, and every person in the thousand who watched could see the visible devil in the eyes and in the quivering ears of the great horse. Clancy meant mischief and showed it. And here was not even a normal man—here was a cripple who had come down to engage him in hand-to-hand combat!

When the crowd parted and opened a pathway for him to come up to Doone, the latter frowned down at the little man.

"Well," said he, eyeing the crippled leg and the long staff, "is this here a joke?"

"A joke?" echoed Holden. "Certainly not."

"Where's your saddle, then?"

"This is it."

78

He showed a light little English pigskin pad of a few pounds weight—a negligible thing compared with the towering structures which the cow ponies had to wear when they were being broken or when they were being worked. It was a badly worn second-hand affair, and the big man shook his head and smiled.

"You're gunna sit on top of Clancy—in that!"

"In this," said Holden gently but firmly.

"All right," said he. "This is your own funeral. I ain't payin' the bills for damages, you know, old-timer. Go to it. I'll tell the boys to get that there leather postage stamp that you call a saddle onto Clancy. Unless Clancy makes a pass at it and swallers it by mistake."

"Thank you," said Holden. "But I'll manage my own saddling."

"*You* will?" gasped out Doone. "You mean that you'll saddle Clancy all by yourself? No help? No nothin'?"

"No, nothing," said Holden, smiling. "Except that I'd like to have people a little farther back. Ten steps back from the fence will keep them close enough to see everything that happens. But it'll keep 'em from scaring Clancy to death every time they lift a hand or speak."

Nothing could have been a simpler request. But it was difficult to execute. Those along the fence had, many of them, waited for hours, standing there to keep their prize positions to wait for the fight to begin. Now they protested bitterly as they were worked back to the required distance. And finally all was prepared.

"The folks is standin' back about the way you want, Holden," said Doone. "And there's Clancy waitin' for you. I hope that they ain't nothin' holdin' you back none?"

"Not a thing!" said Holden, and he advanced toward the corral.

"He may be a man-killer, but he's mighty scared of that hoss!" was the comment of one buckaroo, and there was no doubt that he was right, for the complexion of Holden was a sickly thing as he advanced.

He reached the fence, and there he paused for a long time, waiting, leaning upon his staff and upon the fence. The crowd was perfectly patient. It was watching a man about to attempt the impossible. Therefore this long pause was filled with a heartbreaking tenseness of suspense, as when the players line up on the playing field, but the whistle has not yet blown.

The stallion, in the meantime, stood in the exact center of the corral, paying no apparent heed to anything, squarely facing the cripple, and with his ears flat along his neck. Then Holden, stooping, dragged himself through the fence, between the bars, and stood up, helping himself to an erect position with his staff, and the wretched little saddle dragging down under one arm.

There was a shrill-pitched gasp from the crowd. That breath of dismay came from the women, whose nerves had been brought to a fine edge of terror and horror.

And even Alexa, steady as a balance wheel as a rule, caught at the arm of her father.

"Dad," she whispered, "that great brute will smash him to bits! I can see it in his eyes! Ready—to kill him—Dad!"

For the stallion had lifted its head, suddenly, and arched its crest a little, a certain sign that it was about to come into action.

"Steady, Alexa," said the father as calmly as he could, though his own heart was beating like a triphammer with the horrible excitement of the moment. "That youngster is not a fool. He's a very clever young chap, and he won't be in that corral unless he knows a way to get out safely."

"But if he's murdered—"

"It will be a grisly thing! However, I wish to the Lord that I hadn't come to watch the affair—that boy can't move fast enough to save himself from being ruined, in case Clancy goes bad. And he's sure to go bad. And yet—heaven bless my soul!"

He uttered his last exclamation as the stallion, after advancing a step or two, suddenly paused again and shook his head. Then—a sign of peace as sure as a rainbow in heaven—the ears of the great horse pricked up and forward. And there was a sigh of breathless relief from the horrified watchers.

"Thank God!" breathed Alexa.

And then her father added, what was the thought of the entire group of the spectators: "What in thunder has happened to Clancy?"

16

No ONE CAN look at a miraculous happening without turning to a neighbor for a confirming glance. So it was with the crowd which watched Tom Holden in the ring with the stallion. And by the time that stir and muttering of wonder had ended, Tom Holden slipped the saddle over the back of the great animal. Behold! He leaned far beneath the monster and caught the cinch which dangled from the farther flap of the saddle. Now what a chance for Clancy to rend this fragile bit of humanity to bits! No—he merely turned his head and sniffed the shoulder of Holden while the latter drew up the cinch as tight as he could. And if Clancy disliked the biting cincture of that girth, he showed it merely by shaking his head.

The bridle next. How would he put the bit between those teeth? Very simply! He took the man-killer by the mane and led it to the fence. Then he clambered up to the first rail, and he was then tall enough to reach to the ears of the great stallion. Yes, over those ears Clancy allowed the bridle to be slipped. And the teeth which had closed more than once on human flesh allowed themselves to be pried apart while the bit was inserted! The whole population of the town of Larramee stood by and groaned with astonishment. This was like walking on water or handling fire unscathed. Only, it was a greater miracle, for they knew more about Clancy than they did about water and fire as destroyers.

There was more to come. He must mount to the saddle,

81

and this was quite a different proposition. Twice the cripple lifted his weak leg and put the foot in the stirrup. Twice Clancy, whirling suddenly, sent the poor youth reeling and staggering, but still he returned to the work. Not once did the suspense slacken. For now Clancy seemed to be wakening to the possibility of the situation. Before this, he had been as one drugged, indeed. Now the familiar gleam was coming back into his eyes and his ears flicked back and forth as the shadowy passions rose and ebbed in his soul.

But at length he permitted himself to be led up to the fence and waited there until the slender form of Tom Holden was safely ensconced on his back—like a pigmy on a mountain top. And very plainly Holden was afraid. That could be seen in his staring eyes and in his white, drawn face, and by the tremor of his hands. He was in deadly peril, and he knew it.

Clancy, in the meantime, though his ears had been up the moment before, as soon as this burden dropped onto his back, turned into a devil. His ears flattened, his eyes rolled wickedly, and he crouched to tenseness, ready for a spring. There was but one instant of wire-drawn tautness. Then he vaulted into the air and landed on his stiffened front legs. True sun-fishing!

It would have taken a good rider to sit through that single jump. It would have been very strange if a cripple could have withstood it. And Holden was not equal to this necessary miracle. He was snapped from the saddle like a pebble from a boy's thumb. He landed with an audible thud and rolled over and over in the thick dust of the corral, while Clancy, whirling like a fiend incarnate, lunged after his late rider.

A dozen guns flashed in the sun at the same instant, but never a bullet could have been in time to stop that charge had not Clancy swerved at the last moment and leaped across the prostrate form. Then around the corral he whirled, his ears flat, his eyes full of hell fire, his tail lashing as an angry cat's, his mighty hoofs shaking the ground. That would have been his last moment in life, for it seemed plain that he was working himself into a frenzy before smashing the cripple to bits, but at this instant, Tom Holden propped himself up on one shaking hand and raised the other.

The impact of the fall had started a stream of crimson from his nose, and his eyes were dull with the shock. They could hardly believe their ears when they heard him say: "No guns, friends! This is between Clancy and me!"

Between a dwarf and a giant, a lamb and a lion!

However, they stayed their hands. Yonder raged the stallion like a cat which has missed a mouse. Except that, in this case, the mouse had not escaped. No, though Holden dragged himself uneasily to his feet and staggered as he stood, he made no effort to escape from the impending danger.

Then Clancy charged. High above that frail form he reared, and Alexa covered her eyes.

"Look!" said her father.

She looked again. The man was not down. Clancy had changed his mind; the magic was working again, and yonder was Holden leading him toward the fence once more! Poor Tom Holden, covered with thick dust, his face smudged with crimson, leading the monster calmly toward the fence and leaning heavily on the mane of the stallion!

There at the fence he mounted once more. The sheriff himself thought fit to take a hand at this point.

"Holden," he said, "you've done very well, and like a brave chap. But there ain't no use goin' any further. We've all seen you're as game as they come. But this time he'll murder you! Don't try it again."

Words seemed to fail Holden, or perhaps he was too weak to answer, for it could be plainly seen that the effect of the fall had told terribly upon his delicate body. There was still in his eyes a blank stare of concentrated agony and effort, and his body was bowed in the saddle.

Once more, as his weight slipped into the stirrups, Clancy crouched. He started a sudden step forward, and even that small jar unbalanced the rider and sent him sprawling along the neck of the giant horse. It was so absurd that a boy in the crowd burst into laughter. Something in that note of mirth shocked even that hardy lot of spectators, and a strong hand laid the merry youth in the dirt.

In the meantime the others saw the stallion stop short and turn his head, not to tear Holden with his teeth, but to sniff in kindly inquiry at the half-fallen form of his rider, as though wondering what could have unseated him. They saw, also, how Holden slowly, with a groan of effort, drew himself back into the saddle and sat there perspiring with anguish.

Then Clancy went on again, but softly, softly, with his head turned a little to watch every move of the man on his back. At the fence he was turned by a touch of the reins.

"What shall I do?" asked Tom Holden. "Is he ridden now?"

"Get off," said Doone with some emotion. "That hoss is yours, son, and you've well earned him, and them that say you rode that hoss with dope in him lies. We've seen him work. Get off, Holden. Clancy belongs to you."

Holden replied to that announcement and to the uproar of the crowd with a faint smile and a gesture. He took one foot from the stirrup and slid down. Only by gripping at Clancy did he save himself from falling. Then he clambered through the fence once more and picked up his staff. Men and children swarmed about him to shake his hand and shower him with praise, but Holden waved them back, and through their midst came a tall, gaunt form which they all feared: Aunt Carrie, striding like a man.

She put an arm around the sinking body of Holden. "Can you walk, child?" said she in her harsh voice.

"I can walk—fine," said Holden. "But keep 'em out of my path!"

She cleared them away with a few stinging words, and so she brought him to the hotel again and helped him up the stairs to his room. At the threshold he dropped suddenly to the floor, but Aunt Carrie waved back the dozen strong hands which proffered to raise him. She herself gathered him in her long, bony arms and bore him to the bed. Then she opened his shirt and felt his heart.

"He's still living," she announced to the crowd, "no thanks to you, the lot of you that would have seen him killed and laughed about it afterward. Now go get him the doctor, and get him quick!"

The doctor was brought; he was already hurrying to the spot, indeed.

Afterward, when he was gone, and Aunt Carrie was left alone in the room with the invalid, the doctor came out and talked to the curious crowd in the lobby of the hotel. He was a young doctor; he was succeeding in Larramee because he could handle a rope and a gun as well as a surgeon's knife.

"Is he bad hurt?" asked the sheriff.

"Not a broken bone, and no internal injuries. It's what I'd call shock," said the doctor. "Not the shock of hitting the ground so much as a mental strain of some kind, which finally snapped. He'll be all right by tomorrow morning."

"What sort of strain, doctor?" asked one. "Kind of strain that comes from riding around at night and sticking up stray gents?"

There was deep, mirthless laughter, at this, but the doctor shook his head. "It looked to me," said he, "as though that was the first horse he ever rode."

"How did he do it, then?"

"I'm darned if I know," said the doctor gravely. "I've never believed in the hypnotism of humans, let alone horses!"

In the meantime, Holden opened his eyes and found above him the cracked ceiling of the hotel room.

"Are you better, Tom Holden?" asked the voice of the witch.

He tried to lift himself in the bed, but she pressed him back.

"Steady," said she. "You've ridden Clancy. It's all over. But tell me how under heaven you managed it?"

"It was very easy," said Holden in a faint voice.

"Easy?" she echoed.

"Certainly," said he, managing a smile. "You see, Clancy was waiting for a real man. That was all!"

"Man?" said Aunt Carrie. "Bah! I'd make two such men!"

But she spoke without sufficient emphasis, and all the while, without her knowledge, perhaps, she was patting the hand of Holden with her long, bony fingers.

17

MR. JOHN CUTTING had sent a telegram ahead of him. Therefore he was met at the railroad station near Larramee by none other than the great Oliphant Larramee in person. There was no servant; and the blooded pair of chestnuts which Mr. Larramee drove to the rubber-tired buggy would hardly stand at a hitching rack. Indeed, when the train came in, it took all the skill of Larramee with voice and hand and whip to keep them from jumping through their collars or smashing themselves into the nearest barbed-wire fence. So, when the engine at last stood still, panting and quivering, Larramee backed the horses toward the platform and called aloud to Cutting. The latter recognized with a start the big man under the linen duster. When he had last seen Larramee, that gentleman had been dressed in a far different fashion. Besides, it was not for the face of the father that young Cutting was keeping so close a lookout. And a shadow of surprise and of dismay crossed his brow as he observed the older man. He hurried toward him, a big carry-all valise in one hand and a smaller suitcase in the other, yet swinging both of them easily, for Cutting was not so long out of the university that his shoulders had forgotten their strength.

He swung them into the rear of the rig. Then he swung himself lightly over the wheel and into the seat beside Larramee.

"You don't mind horses?" said Larramee, settling the near one of his span with a steady voice and checking rein.

"I like 'em. Ridden all my life."

"Riding is one thing. Driving is another. These days of automobiles, more people have ridden a horse than ever sat behind the beauties and looked at their switching tails. But—I prefer flesh to take me over the ground. Well—here goes!"

With this, he loosed the reins an imperceptible trifle, and though he still leaned a little forward in the seat, his thick arms well extended along the narrow leather strips to maintain a stout pull on the bits, the pair leaped forward with one consent. That first lurch took young Cutting by surprise. Automobiles do not start on wings. Moreover, after he had been flattened against the seat, he had other things, immediately, to take up his attention. In six strides those fine trotters were hitting a two-forty gait, which even translated into automobile terms is twenty-five miles an hour. This through the crowded traffic of horses, automobiles, carts, and pedestrians around the station. The mighty wrists of Larramee turned them back and forth. They shaved vehicles and lives by scant fractions of inches on either side, and then they straightened out into the one long main street of Larramee. Here, though the pace had even increased, Larramee sat back in his seat as though the excitement was over. With leveled, flagging ears, with harness flopping loose and high over the quick pulsations of the driving hips, with noses stretched eagerly ahead, that pair of wild young horses tore down the main thoroughfare of Larramee, darted around a corner at a rate that made the rear wheels of the buggy skid wildly, and straighten off again onto a country road which pointed toward a distant hill and a big house surmounting it. By this time Cutting had recovered his nerve and his breath. And he was able to smile a little askance at the impassive face of the retired millionaire.

"Alexa wanted to come down for you," said Larramee, in answer to that look. "But she wanted to drive these horses, and I wouldn't let her. Safe, of course. Gentle as lambs when you're used to them."

"I quite understand," murmured Cutting, turning a little pale at the thought. "Certainly it would be rash to risk any woman in the world behind these young—devils."

"She likes speed," said Larramee. "When I told her she had to take the browns, she sulked. That's why I'm down here."

"Very good of you, sir," said Cutting. "That's Alexa, of course."

And he ventured a short laugh, pitched rather uneasily high; for he was not very well acquainted with Larramee. He wanted to ingratiate himself, but he was also very much afraid of this famous man.

"That's Alexa," said Larramee, without the qualifying smile. "She hasn't broken her neck yet. Two or three years more, however—well, I never could understand where she gets it!"

This was a twisted span between two deeply gouged ruts, either of which was deep and stiff enough to have snapped off a wheel at the axle. Cutting bit his lip and said nothing.

"Her mother was always a gentle soul," said Larramee. "And I think I bear the reputation of a quiet man, Alexa is a throwback to some rough ancestor. There have been a few wild Larramees, you know."

Mr. Cutting listened and controlled himself by blinking hard, straight at the sun. He was remembering certain tales which his own father had told him of this same Oliphant Larramee smashing and crashing his way through the wrecks of other fortunes on Wall Street and carving out amusement and new millions for himself. Yet he seemed to consider himself a gentle spirit!

But all of this talk was calling up in his mind the radiant picture of Alexa Larramee, and the heart of Cutting swelled in him. He could not keep back the question which was big in his mind.

"There is a rumor in New York," said he, "that Alexa is to marry a man—let me see—Holden, I think it is."

He dared not look at Larramee, for fear the rancher would notice the pallor of his face. But there was no response for a moment.

"Rumors travel fast," said Larramee at last.

This was scant satisfaction. And the fears of Cutting suddenly redoubled.

"It's true, then?" he asked with a sudden sharpness.

There was so much in his voice that Larramee glanced at him and smiled a little.

"I don't know," said he. "Alexa has her own way, very much of the time. Just what her intentions may be, I cannot answer."

"But," cried the other, "the same rumor has it that this Holden is a marauder—a good deal of a rascal, in fact. Of course that can't be true!"

"I only know," said Larramee, smiling more broadly than ever, "that he is the most impertinent youngster I have ever met in my life! I can answer, too, that his nerve is as good as steel."

"He's young, then?"

"Very. Not more than twenty-one or two, I should say."

"A brilliant young robber, a fighter—perhaps Alexa has grown romantic about him?"

"I have not the slightest idea," answered the rancher, drawing the horses to a walk as they began the steep grade of the hill. "You must ask Alexa herself all about it. As I said before, and as you must know for yourself, she has her own mind and her own determinations. I should never dream of trying to influence her in any really important matter such as a husband!"

There was a vein of bitterness underlying this which made Mr. Cutting thoughtful, and he recalled another rumor— how many and how fast-feathered are such tales about the figure of a rich man's house and a pretty girl—to the effect that having once gone to great trouble in picking out a husband for his daughter, Mr. Larramee had the painful embarrassment of having his choice rejected at the last moment. This, no doubt, had something to do with his attitude in the present matter.

They reached the house. It looked smaller from the level beside it than it did from the valley below where Larramee itself lay. Indeed, it was a most modest place for the home of so rich a man. It was surrounded by a haphazard garden of random trees, intermixed with irregular splotches of lawn, of hedge flowers, and of wild blossoms sown in profusion and carelessness. And the building behind this screen of cool greenery and color was a rambling collection of additions to what had once been a hunting lodge. From the distance it looked a good deal like a small castle. Close at hand it more resembled a country summer hotel, and not a very good one at that! It was all timber. It was not freshly painted, and in place of paint, vines had been allowed to grow where they would. In some places they cast long green trailers through the windows and into the interior of the house. Here and there the arms had found a better footing around the windows and had quite blotted out an entire light so that the room within must be both dark and hot. But in their fantasies, these vines had not been disturbed. They were allowed to do as they would. Some of them sprawled close along the ground. Others twisted along halfway ledges; others again had worked up to the very roof and there, seeming to gain new life with the hot sun just above them, had spilled forth quantities of streamers which showered across the roofing and dropped far beneath the eaves in streamers and cool festoons.

John Cutting had only a moment to observe these things, for through an archway in the garden Alexa herself came hurrying toward him. Servants took his bags; Mr. Larramee whirled away toward the stables, which were at a little distance; and here he was with a feeling that he had crossed the continent on seven-league boots. It was unbelievable that she was actually before him, more brown of face than when he had last seen her, and her eyes a richer blue, he thought.

They spent five minutes on old mutual friends. But a fish cannot swim idly with a hook in its mouth, and Cutting, in agony, had to talk of the matter which was most in his mind.

"I came across the continent," said he bluntly, at last, "with just one object, Alexa."

He paused a moment to gather courage, and she looked

rather anxiously at him, to see whether or not it was necessary to change the subject, but since he had proposed to her, already, three times, it seemed absurd that he would rush some two thousand miles to ask her the same question over again.

"It's about the matter of this man Holden," said he. "I heard—"

Alexa stamped. "You heard wrong!" she cried.

"Thank heaven!" sighed Mr. Cutting. "I really thought it was impossible—a person no one had ever heard of—and trailing a reputation which was not exactly a cloud of glory—"

"Do you mean to say," she asked, "that they are talking about him even in—"

"Even back there," he said.

"I wish he were dead," she answered, with a fierceness which delighted the soul of John Cutting.

"So do I," he admitted. "However, it seems that he's the next best thing. He really—"

"He really is a low person I have never met. Reputation? Why, John, it's said that he's a midnight robber!"

"We heard something to the same effect. I was afraid, for a moment that—"

"Not seriously!"

"You're so infernally impulsive, Alexa! I've been in hell, frankly, for a week."

"How much talk?"

"This much." He drew out a newpaper clipping. It was headed with a four-column picture of the lovely face of Alexa.

"That ridiculous bathing suit again!" said Alexa, flushing. Then she added, as she read the headlines: "Oh, John, the whole world must know!"

"I suppose so."

"What are they saying? Oh, they must be laughing—"

"Not at all. Everyone felt at once that this Holden must be an unusual man."

"He is!"

"Yes?" Cutting inquired with alarm.

"An unusual villain. He dared to announce that he expected to become my husband. Think of it!"

"But your father, Alexa! I should think that Oliphant

90

Larramee would have him coated with tar and feathers, and—"

"So should I, if I'd been a man. But you never can understand what Dad will do. He's so impulsive. So wild himself. He actually hasn't raised a hand!"

"I can't understand—"

"Hush! Here is Dad now. And there's mischief in his eye."

"How can you tell?"

"By his smile. That always means trouble."

Oliphant Larramee came slowly toward them, taking off his linen duster.

"You have a pleasant surprise coming, my dear," said he.

"What is that?"

"A gentleman is riding toward the house to see you."

"What gentleman, Dad?"

"Mr. Thomas Holden."

"Dad!"

"I thought I'd prepare you, my dear."

"Oh!" cried Alexa. "Do you mean that you'll actually let me see him?"

"In fact," said Oliphant Larramee, "I've agreed to introduce him!"

18

At that instant, as Alexa and Cutting started to their feet, the sun winked far off, down the slope, upon the sleek hide of a blood-bay horse.

"John," said she, "come with me to the house."

"If you wish to be sheltered from this—Holden," said the latter, his square jaw thrusting out in fine style, "I should be delighted to accommodate you, Alexa."

"Hush!" she cried, capturing his hand and drawing him along. "You don't understand. He's a terrible person—thinks nothing of taming wild horses, or of killing men. God knows how many murders are to his credit."

"This is the twentieth century, Alexa," said John Cutting. "They hang such fellows nowadays!"

"This is the twentieth century," she agreed with a sigh, "but it's not New York. And in this part of the country they are very hard on all sorts of crimes except the worst of them all. Gun fights are looked on as fist fights are looked on in your part of the country."

She said this as she got safely inside the house. Then she faced him.

"What am I going to do?" she asked breathlessly.

"I don't know. I wish to heaven—but Mr. Larramee—"

"I know you're confused, John. You wonder what's in the mind of Dad. I wonder too. But I have a terrible surmise. I don't dare to tell you!"

"You'd better. If I can help you, Alexa—"

"It's a crazy tangle of suspicions. I only know that Dad rushed down to the town one day to destroy this rascal, and that he came back without doing it. You know that my father has a reputation of doing what he starts out for. What made him fail here?"

"If this fellow is a gun fighter—"

"That's not it. Dad would storm a fort, if he felt that his family's honor dictated such a thing. That's not it. Besides, he has only to raise his hand in the town and twenty men would be behind him to do what he asks them to do. No, it's something else. And now he allows this man to come to the house, and insists on introducing him to me—in person! After I've been insulted so publicly—"

She threw out both her hands in a gesture of despair and of anguish. "Don't you see, John?"

"I'm bewildered, Alexa. It doesn't seem real or possible. Not with Oliphant Larramee!"

"I know. There's only one way to explain it. You know that Dad has led a romantic, strange sort of a life. He's done all manner of things in his time. Suppose that one of those things was—not an honest or honorable affair? Suppose this Thomas Holden, in some way, got hold of it? Suppose that that knowledge was what lay behind his public statement that he intended to marry me? And suppose—suppose that's the club with which he's compelling my father to go so far—"

"In the name of heaven, Alexa, do you believe all of this?"

"What other explanation is there?"

92

"With such a serious hold—he could even—"

"Try to force me to marry him? That's what I've kept awake at night wondering about."

"You wouldn't do it, Alexa?"

"To save Dad's honor? I'd go through fire for him!"

At this, John Cutting grew deathly pale. He could not speak for a moment. "Go to your room," he urged at last. "Refuse to meet him. Afterward, I'll try to talk to him."

"And be pistoled without remorse or conscience? I tell you, John, this Holden is a remarkable person. He is a slender little cripple—the gentlest-appearing soul in the world. His voice is as soft as a child's voice. But in reality, he's a devil. You know when opposites go together they make the worst poisons. It's that way with Holden. He's apparently one of those natural fiends who delight in murder for its own sake. I tell you frankly, John, that if you ever face him with so much as a frown, he'll kill you out of hand!"

She added: "As for running away to my room—if my father is cornered and helpless, do you think that I'll help to put a gun to his head?"

Even John Cutting, with all the schemes of a lover rushing through his brain, could think of nothing to say. He bowed his head, and they went on together into the living room, and they sat down in the farthest corner.

From that position, though they had chosen it accidentally, they could see Thomas Holden ride up and confront Larramee in the open driveway. They could see a great ragged wolf dog lie down under the nose of the horse and snarl silently up at the millionaire, they could see Holden take a long staff which he balanced across the pommel of the saddle, and so clamber down to the ground with infinite pain. In this way, leaning on the staff, he faced Larramee.

"Holden," said the big man, "this affair has started as a joke. It has developed into something else. You have taken up a chance word which I dropped. If I live up to my contract, I shall be forced to insult my daughter under her own roof. I had rather cut off an arm!" He added: "Think this over, Holden!"

Holden, indeed, bowed his pale face toward the ground in quiet meditation.

"I have thought it over from first to last," he said at length. "And it is worth while."

"In what way, man? You come into my house. You are presented to my daughter—if I can persuade her to come down and see you. She rises and leaves the room. Then you have succeeded in offending her, in mortally insulting me, and where is your gain?"

"All of this is true," said Holden. "I have thought of it all. All!"

"My own opinion," said Larramee slowly, "you do not value."

"On the contrary," said Holden, "I value it more than the opinion of any man I have ever known."

"Bah!" said Larramee. "That is simply noisesome flattery."

"If you will think for a moment," said Holden, "you will see that I have not the slightest reason to flatter you. I am not a fool. I realize that nothing can change your scorn or your hatred for me!"

At this, the rich man was staggered. There is such a thing as golden sincerity, the sound of which is current coin in every ear with wit enough to distinguish between good and bad. And here was sincerity of such a nature. Mr. Larramee reconsidered Tom Holden. The more he saw of the phases of this youth, the harder he found it to reconcile them with one another and make a comprehensible whole.

"Very well," said Larramee at last. "We will not argue about that point. I have a very definite and concrete offer to make you. What your scheme is with me and with my daughter I cannot tell. I grant that you are a confident and clever chap. But you must be aware that I myself am not a complete idiot. If you take my proposal, all is well. If you do not, I shall do my best to crush you, Holden, and you must be aware that I have tools at my disposal."

Holden drew in a long breath. "The whole town and the countryside is under your thumb. I understand it perfectly," said he.

"Very well, Holden. You have fulfilled one part of a foolish bargain which I made with you. You have ridden a wild horse up to my house. It is your right to claim that I fulfill my contract, take you into that house, and do my best to introduce you to my daughter. At the same time, you will win the full weight of my enmity. This is one part of the bargain and one aspect of the thing, is it not?"

"It is, sir."

"The other is that you take in hand a check for a certain sum of money and leave the town of Larramee and never come back."

Holden bowed, and his face turned a sicker white than ever.

"Well?" asked Larramee sharply. "You understand? We need not mince words with one another. I have been a rough-handed fellow in my day, and by the gods, if the occasion arose I could be rough handed again. But I have enough money to keep me from certain of the frictions of life. I don't choose to act unless I am compelled to it. Now, Holden, balancing my enmity against whatever cash gains you have in mind in this adventure of yours—which at present seems to consist in heaping as much shame on the head of my daughter as possible—balancing one thing against the other—don't you think that it would be wise to take a check for, say, a thousand dollars, and take yourself off to another climate?"

Holden looked into his face sadly, gravely. Then he shook his head. "I cannot agree with you," said he.

"I beg your pardon," said Larramee. "I misjudged you, quite. I see that you are a man of caliber, Holden. I will offer you five thousand dollars on the spot. In exchange, you will never show yourself near my house again and you will never, under whatever circumstances, mention her name?"

Holden looked about him blankly. It was a bright, peaceful day. Little transparent wisps of cloud stood in the sky, too thin to make a shadow of the torrents of sunshine which rained through to the earth. A squirrel ran boldly out to the tip of a branch of a tree beside him. There was nothing that he could use as a sample and an illustration of what he felt.

"I can only say," said he, "that if you offered fifty thousand, or five hundred thousand, it could not buy me off."

Larramee nodded. "I hardly expected that I could do it," he said thoughtfully. "This will be a black day in your record of life, my young friend. Tell me only this. What do you expect to gain which will be of more solid value to you than five thousand in cash?"

And Holden answered quietly: "The inexpressible happiness of seeing her, of standing before her, of speaking so that she must hear me—and of hearing her speak in exchange!"

"Folderol and nonsense!" snapped out the great man.

19

IT WAS THE first well-furnished room in which Holden had ever entered. He had tethered the stallion outside; the wolf dog, Sneak, followed him to the entrance to the house and there lay down across the threshold, on guard, ready to take advantage of any opening for the work of mischief which was ever nearest and dearest to his heart. And Holden, advancing without this escort, felt strangely alone.

He was only dimly aware of a few physical objects near him. There were two things or three which had a distant reality to him. One was the solid yellow arm of sunshine which, thrust through a window, turned a crimson cluster of window flowers to flame, and descended upon the bold pattern of the rug. The second object was the face of Alexa in the distance, pale as a ghost, and—oh, far unlike the painting which hung in the house of the witch.

He made his way cautiously with his staff. Once the rough wooden point was all that saved him from falling as a small runner slipped beneath his feet. As he went forward, he took note of another thing. Mr. Larramee showed not the slightest vexation. From his conversation beforehand, it was very plain that he was raging with anger within. But he maintained an exterior of the most perfect indifference.

Holden, noting this, decided that the great man was greater than report had painted him, and far more dangerous.

"Alexa," he said, "I have come to present to you an

acquaintance of mine, Mr. Thomas Holden. Mr. Holden, this is my daughter, Miss Larramee."

He added: "And this is my friend, Mr. John Cutting. You will excuse me for a moment, Mr. Holden?"

With this he was gone from the room and left poor Tom Holden face to face with the most terrible of all powers—an injured woman. She smiled upon him coldly; then she turned to John Cutting.

"We are happy to have Mr. Holden with us," she said. "Perhaps you have not heard that Mr. Holden is a famous wit?"

"I have not," admitted Cutting, and he fastened a formidable pair of bold, staring eyes upon the other, as though trying to search out by this diligent inquiry the secret which made the slender young cripple so formidable, even to a man like the celebrated Oliphant Larramee. He could not find what he searched for. To all appearances this was no more than a weakling, a fellow not worth regarding for a moment.

"His last jest was very amusing," said Alexa. "He announced himself as my future husband. At a dance, John."

"I hope," said Cutting, "that there was a great deal of laughter?"

Holden felt himself burned to the heart with this contempt, this scornful sarcasm. And yet how could he reply? Certainly not to her; but here was a man before him, and to uphold his reputation, he must make some answer.

"Of course," said he gently to the girl, "it is your privilege to say what you please. I wanted to come here to make an explanation. I suppose you don't care to hear it?"

"You are delightfully naive, Mr. Holden," said Alexa, and rose from her chair. "But I confess that this is a very busy day with me."

Even Holden, unskilled as he was in social manners and customs, could not fail to take so broad a hint. He bowed to her, with his hat still under his arm, leaning heavily on the staff.

"I shall find another time for that explanation," he said, growing whiter than before.

"Your other visits," said Alexa bitterly, "will of course be arranged through my father."

"If you please."

"I do," said she.

"Good-by, Miss Larramee."

"Good-by, Mr. Holden."

"Shall I see Mr. Holden out?" asked Cutting.

"No, no, John!" And she caught at his arm. At this, the head of Holden went up and a spot of color leaped into his cheeks.

"It will be easy to remember you, too, Mr. Cutting."

That taunt was too much for the vigorous spirit of John Cutting. He stepped forward. No matter how dire might be the powers of the cripple as a gunfighter, he would endure no slight in the presence of the girl.

"I hope you do, Holden," he said grimly. "I shall keep you in mind, also. Particularly on account of your jests, and your manner of using Miss Larramee's name in public."

"John!" cautioned the girl. "That's more than necessary! Be careful."

"Confound it, Alexa," cried Cutting, "this man mustn't presume that he can look me down, no matter what his record as a gunman and murderer may be. Mr. Larramee may not choose to speak his mind to you, Holden. I'll speak mine instead—"

"Hush, John!" cried the girl.

"I won't be quiet about it, Alexa. By Jove, it eats into me like an acid. These things can't be put up with, you know. It's not honorable to pocket up such things. It really isn't! Mr. Holden, you have acted like a cad and cur toward Miss Larramee, and the next time I see you, if I have a riding whip with me, I'll give you my opinion in something stronger than words."

There poured over Tom Holden all the horror of his weakness, all the sense of the overpowering strength of this athletic young man, all the shame of this scene in the very face of the girl. There was nothing left for him except to fall back upon the vague power of words and that false reputation which had been built up around him, like a mystery which has no foundation.

"Mr. Cutting," said he, "you talk very well—before ladies."

That taunt snapped the restraint of Cutting. He was a fellow of strong impulses, always, and the striking muscles of his good right arm had been taut ever since he first heard the name and the exploits of Mr. Holden. It was quite against his will. He did not wish to do such a thing in such a place. But

98

his fist acted of its own accord, suddenly. It flicked out and struck the terrible Tom Holden squarely on the face and crashed him to the floor while the staff fell with a great rattling a long distance away.

It amazed Cutting. He had been used to boxing with men of his own heavyweight dimensions, where a fist found a solid lodgment. This blow of his striking had not possessed half of his power, but it was as though he had aimed it at little Alexa Larramee. Holden had gone down as lightly as that.

"His gun, John!" screamed the girl.

That thought was in Cutting at the same moment. He could actually prevision the draw of the long Colt and hear the speaking of the revolver, and feel the heavy slug tear through his flesh. He was upon Holden in a single bound and had him by the nape of the neck.

"You rat!" snarled out Cutting in an ecstasy of rage and power, like a fighting dog which had sunk its teeth home in a death hold.

And here was Holden, limp in his hands; but Holden had an ally which came now in a whirl and a streak—a bounding gray streak which slipped across the threshold of the room and went at Cutting silently, its murderous fangs bared. The scream of Alexa was too late. There was no time for Cutting to spring away and defend himself. It was the voice of Holden which stopped the brute and brought it to a sliding halt at the side of its master, head flattened close to the floor, legs crouched and prepared, its whole wicked soul showing in green fire in its eyes. Cutting had leaped back. He would not run and leave Alexa behind him to face the crazed brute. But he was very close to a panic. Holden, in the meantime, dropped again by Cutting, had propped himself up, gathered the staff, and raised himself slowly to his feet. A little trickle of red was slowly running down from his mouth. Now he drew out a white handkerchief and pressed it over the bleeding place. Then he nodded to Cutting and smiled on him in a way that made the flesh of that healthy youth creep.

"You are a brave man, Cutting," he said, "and a strong man, too. But the next time we meet, I shall come prepared for you. I do not fight with my hands, Mr. Cutting. And when I see you again, I shall have other weapons. Steady, boy," he added to the dog, which had begun to work itself forward on its belly, slavering with eagerness to be at the throat of the other. "Good-by, Miss Larramee."

He turned and went from the room slowly, hobbling painfully, for he had fallen on his weak leg.

"The devil," murmured big John Cutting. "I feel as though he had knocked *me* down. Confound him, Alexa. I beg your pardon a thousand times for allowing all of this to happen in your house and before you—but I couldn't help it—my hand simply shot out of its own accord."

He turned to Alexa and found that she was still staring before her, as though she still saw violent action unrolling itself in her view.

"The dog could have torn you to bits, John. Did you notice that?"

"He looked quite able to."

"Why did Holden call him off?"

"It's a nasty mess, all of it. I don't understand anything."

"Nor I," whispered Alexa.

"You see, Alexa, you hadn't prepared me for this. I thought the fellow was a pure scoundrel. A rascally sneaking, murderous villain with a gun under each hand."

"But he had no weapon with him!"

"Do you think that? It wasn't that he was afraid—"

"Afraid?" cried the girl. "No, no! He may be everything that's vile. But I know what he's done. With my own eyes I've seen how he handled that man-killing Clancy. No, no, John, if he'd wanted to, he could have shot you to bits while he was falling to the floor. But he wouldn't wear a gun when he came to call—on me!"

"After all, Alexa, the man is no good. There's no use being so stricken about it."

"How can you be sure? I thought he was the lowest of the low. I thought he had come up here to put some sort of pressure on me, about Dad, but—John, the terrible part of it is that he acted like a gentleman! And we acted like—what?"

THE EYES OF Oliphant Larramee missed nothing. And though the cripple was already mounted on the great height of the red stallion, he saw at a glance the stricken look on the face of Holden and the stain of blood on his mouth. So he asked with a smile: "Has everything been as pleasant as you expected, Holden?"

He was surprised when the latter managed to smile back at him, even though the effort was manifest.

"As well as could be expected," said he. "I came to learn. But I have had to be a tutor."

"In what, if you please?" asked the rancher.

"Manners," said Holden, and smiled again.

"You taught at some cost, it seems," said the rancher, and stared at the bloodstain.

"These small things," said Holden, "must be endured. Life, it appears, is full of accidents."

"Very well," said the rancher. "I like this spirit in you, Holden. I almost regret, in fact, that you have forced me into a hostile camp with your absurd behavior. In the meantime, what is the next thing I can do for you?"

The smile of Holden turned to a grin. "Ask me to your house again," said he. "For dinner and the night, Mr. Larramee."

Larramee grinned in turn. "I shall be glad to do that," he said, "when the sky falls, or," he added with a peculiar sneering emphasis, "when that rascal who is riding the roads about Larramee at night, robbing and murdering, is captured and brought into the hands of justice, and the case proved against him!"

"Is that a bargain?" asked Holden.

"Certainly," said the rancher, shrugging his shoulders. "When that man is brought to justice, I shall be glad to have you in the house as a guest."

"You are very kind," murmured Holden, and so he rode off down the hill, jolting clumsily in the saddle, even despite the silken-smooth gait of the stallion.

He did not pause at the town of Larramee, however. He held straight on past it and rode south and west through that day until he ached with weariness. He paused at a little crossroads village for the night and journeyed again on the following day until the height of the midafternoon. Then he came to his destination. It was a foothills town, or rather it was a conjunction of four or five houses, a schoolhouse, and a store which carried the name of a town.

Of the storekeeper he asked if he could be directed to the place of Christopher Venner. The storekeeper smiled at once, and by that smile revealed that an excellent patron had been named to him. He himself came forth onto the worn veranda and pointed over the hills, whose brown sides were dimmed by a myriad of tangling heat waves. "Over in the valley," he said. "You'll see a big old house with a lump of scrub cypress on one side of it, and a bunch of willows along the creek next to it. That's Venner's place. Might you be a friend of his?"

"I was a friend," said Holden tentatively, "before he struck it rich. Maybe I won't be so thick with him now."

The storekeeper shook his head. He said, looking first at the magnificent form of the red horse: "If you want a job, he'll be the one to get you a place. Or," he added, changing the direction of his glance to the crippled leg of the little man, "if you want a hand-out, he's the gent to fix you up. What he's got, everybody's got, more or less! He's a square shooter, is Venner!"

Holden waited to hear no more, but he spoke to Clancy, and the great horse lifted into a long and swinging gallop which carried his rider lightly toward the hills. From the top of the first low ridge he saw the place. Through a long, narrow valley a stream meandered, here fathered in a yellow pool, there treading out in narrow rapids, a dirty, sullen little creek, but a priceless gift to the rancher, since it meant water for his cows.

The house itself was an old ruin, unpainted, sunwracked and weather-beaten. It looked its feebleness even from the distance. But there were a number of new-built sheds near the house, and yonder was a set of great haystacks to carry the weaker part of the herd through the winter, if the winter should be bad, and the whole valley was dotted, here and there, with the grazing cattle.

In spite of the ancient and tumbledown aspect of the house the valley gave a total impression of great prosperity, and Holden knew that the stolen money of Chris Venner had been put to a good and solid use. He sent the stallion down the slope, therefore, at a round pace, and presently was drawing rein under the enormous mulberry tree which extended its branches before the ranch house.

The nearer view bore out all that he had suspected from the distance. There was prosperity, to be sure, but an utter carelessness of appearance which spoke eloquently of the presence and the directing mind of Chris Venner. In the yard a number of chickens were scratching and the whole surface of the worn garden was pockmarked with their work. In the near distance there was the steady harsh music of swine from the pig pens. In the near pasture were yellow-wooled sheep. Milk cows, a half dozen of them, ambled through another pasture, pleasantly shaded with a scattering of trees, and the whole farm reeked with the air of plenty, and of confusion.

He was looking over this scene when he heard a voice behind him and turned to face Chris Venner in the door of the house. He was not changed an iota. His clothes were even a bit more shabby than they had been when he was on the road. His coat was off, his dirty vest was unbuttoned with the tag of a Bull Durham sack flapping down from it, and he might have been taken any place for a cow-puncher rather than a rancher—a cow-puncher out of luck, at that, and out of work.

He was astonished at the sight of the cripple, too astonished to speak, for a moment. Then he dragged Holden from the horse and almost carried him into the house. His delight was almost pathetic. He planted Holden in a chair and raised a full bellow which brought two Chinese servants running. One was dispatched for cold water from the well; one was sent for whisky. And presently Holden was equipped with his drink. It was old and respectable liquor, but to his unaccustomed taste it was a sort of disgusting fire, which scalded his throat and turned his stomach. Venner poured down his own dram with a single gesture and then dumped out another half tumbler for himself.

"I've been thinkin' of you ten times a day, Holden," he said to the cripple. "The address I give to you, I never thought of you using it. But what's your game in these parts, partner?" he asked, leaning forward and lowering his voice. "What's—"

"You're doing well, here," said Holden.

The other grinned. "I fell into this lucky, old son. Going crooked was hard work. Going straight is a cinch. They ain't nothin' to worry about. All I got to do is work. The devil, man, that's easy. I'm all fixed up. Everything that I've started has turned out extra fine. First place, I came along here and find this here ranch owned by a gent that's quit the West and gone East to live easy—because he struck it rich in the mines, darn his lucky hide! He didn't care what he sold for. It was all auctioned off, from the land to the cows on it. Nobody else around here happened to be very flush. And I raked the whole thing in at about what I wanted to pay for it. I dunno. Maybe it's only worth about twice what I paid for it. But I figger more'n that.

"Then I started lookin' around at the chances on this here place. Nothin' but cows been run on the place for fifty years. Well, old son, cows don't do no harm to ground. They're the makin' of poor soil. And this whole dog-gone valley is rich as a mint if you could get enough rain to farm it. They ain't enough rain, mostly, but they's a lot of water that goes to waste in the creek. I got a smart gent in here from a college, full of talk right out of a book. He showed me pretty pronto where I could slap water out of the river right onto about five hundred acres of bang-up good bottom land. Richer'n gold! So I'm levelin' off that ground. Needed ploughs and harrows and sowers and rakes and sub-soilers, and mowin' machines, and a lot of other junk.

"Well, I went over to the big Crosby ranch, where they was havin' a closing-out sale. I raked in about eight thousand dollars' worth of stuff—it would of cost that new—for about six hundred dollars! You know the way second-hand farm tools go? It'll cost me about fifteen thousand to level off and check up that bottom land; and after that, I got five hundred acres of the finest ground in the world. They'll bring me in seventy-five or a hundred an acre every year of my life. Why, Holden, I'm coinin' money!"

"How much was in that whole clean-up you made from the bank?" asked Holden.

"About fifty-eight thousand, old-timer. A pretty neat lift, eh?"

"Pretty neat," said Holden.

"I've got a few thousand left; after the checking is paid for I'll be in debt, but not for long. Everything is runnin' pretty fine and smooth. I went over to the bank the other day and talks to the president. Can you imagine me settin' down and talkin' to the president of a bank, Holden? There I sat, all swelled up. He gives me a big cigar and lights it for me. 'Put your feet on that chair,' say he, 'and make yourself real easy, Mr. Venner. And what might be your pleasure today, sir,' says he. 'Are you comin' in to pay us a friendly visit, or maybe you are thinkin' of opening business relations with us?'

"Can you get around a bank president talkin' that way to a gent like me, Holden? No, you can't. I sort of gagged, but I managed to keep a straight face.

"'It's partly friendship and partly wantin' to open up business with your bank,' says I.

"'Mr. Venner,' says he, 'I am delighted.'

"He looks me over for a minute, while I aim to get hold of myself and recollect that this here is the same Chris Venner that I always used to know, that never had no money except on the last day of one month and the first day of the next one, him that never could get no credit from nobody for nothin'! I aimed to need, take it all in all, about thirty thousand dollars to clean off the last of the debts agin' the ranch, finish the checkin' up of the ground for the irrigation, putting in the irrigation pump, and lumpin' the whole thing under one head, I seen that twenty-five thousand would be pretty much what I needed. Well, old son, if you know anything about the cow business—which you probably know a pile more than I ever did—you know that a banker always holds his head and makes a little prayer before he loosens up with any money, to a cowman. The cow business is too dog-gone uncertain. One year along comes blackleg and cleans up the cows. The next year there's lots of cows and the prices is so low that it don't

105

hardly pay to ship, and the year after that, they ain't no calves. You understand, I guess?"

"Of course," said the cripple.

"I figgered on all this, but then I says to myself that while he's actin' so mighty generous, I could put up my figgers pretty high. It's always best, you know, to ask about twice what you expect to get. Leastwise, that's been my experience. So I sticks my thumbs into the arm holes of my vest and takes a pull on that there cigar for the sake of gettin' up my courage. When I had worked up a cloud of smoke so's he couldn't watch my face none too close, I says to him, quick and snappy, like it didn't mean nothin' to me: 'About fifty thousand is what I want.'

"He answers right up quick: 'Fifty thousand?' says he. 'If you really need some spare cash, Venner, you'd better make it seventy-five.'

"I batted a hole in that smoke with my hand to have a look at him, but he was squintin' at me as level and serious as though he seen all them little seventy-five thousand greenbacks all printed out in rows with six-per-cent blossoms on their heads every dog-gone year. I couldn't help bustin' out: 'How d'you think that the ranch will stand a tax like that, governor?'

"He just gives me a smile.

" 'Venner,' say he, 'do you suppose that our eyes are shut? We've been watching every move you've made. We know you better than we know a good many men who have been familiar with us half of their lives. The reason is that we've had a chance to see the way your wits work. We've watched you pull in a ranch worth a hundred and a quarter thousand for about fifty thousand. We've watched you buy ten thousand dollars' worth of machinery for a few hundreds, where most of the ranchers were too proud to be in on old, rusty, used stuff, not realizing that it was practically as strong as ever. We've seen you manage your profits without fuss and feathers. You haven't been tearing down the old ranch house and putting up a new one, or even wasting a lot of time and trouble and hard cash painting up the old shack and trying to put a fine face on a bad business. You ain't even bought no furniture—not a stick of it!'

" 'Look here,' says I, 'how come you to be follerin' me so dog-gone close?'

" 'It's our business,' says he. 'Some folks think that a banker only sits down in a chair and figgers out ways to cut the throats of the widows and the orphans and to cheat hard-workin' men out of a livin'. Matter of fact, we have to do everything from detective work to handing out soft soap. Every banker has to try to be a cross between a senator and a servant, and it's mighty hard to hit it right. Most of us are too much one way or the other. I'm letting you in on a ground floor about us,' says he, and he gives me a grin that makes me like him all the way down to the ground, 'partly because you're too smart to put up with any buncombe and partly because I want you to know the worst about us right now, because you're going to do business with this bank the rest of your life, young man, though you may not know it just now.

" 'I say that we've watched you from the start. We know almost to the dollar what your actual needs are. Twenty thousand dollars are about all you want to push you through the pinch. I offer you seventy-five thousand. You wish to know why? In the first place, between you and me, because I wanted to surprise you and make you think that we're a large-landed bank. But as a matter of fact we spend most of our time shaving the outside rims off of dollars to save cents. Then I know that we're well secured even on twice as much as the sum I offered. That irrigated land will be worth not a penny less than four hundred dollars an acre, which means two hundred thousand or nearly a quarter of a million for the lot. Why under heaven none of us ever saw the possibilities in that dirty little yellow river before, I don't know. Let that go. The fact of the matter is that at the present moment I'm willing to hand you seventy-five thousand dollars in cash or credit, whichever you choose. And if you want, I'll make that a hundred thousand, or even a hundred and fifty thousand dollars. Between you and me, there's nothing this bank would like better, young man, than to get its hands on that ranch of yours. Because I have an idea that you can grow fruit trees on that ground, not merely alfalfa. And I have another idea you can expand the irrigated acreage in the valley from five hundred to nine hundred acres.'

" 'By jiminy,' says I, 'you been readin' my mind. Lemme ask you how far back you been follerin' me.'

" 'As far as we cared to,' says he, and he grinned again.

"Holden, that grin of his has been botherin' me a whole lot.

What did he mean by it, d'you think? Was he aimin' to tell me that he knows that I'd been—a crook?" Here Venner lowered his voice and leaned closer.

"Would you care?" asked Holden.

"Would I care? Heaven, yes! It's a hell to me, just the thought of it!"

"You think that they're still working down your back trail?"

"I think just that. And what'll they find out?"

"Not a great deal," said Holden, making a very broad guess. "They'll find a few misdemeanors, a few gun fights, perhaps, and one or two rather shady attempts to make money faster than you ought to. But, on the whole, you never did anything big enough to be called really bad, until you met Blinky Wickson."

Venner poured himself another drink and swallowed it hastily. "They's no use trying to fool you. You know everything about me, Holden. Well, tell me what to do?"

"Would you do it?"

"To get shut of this name of a crook?"

"That's it."

"I'd give the next ten years of my life," breathed Venner. "Oh, I'd give half of the time that's left to me!"

21

THERE IS A strength about passionate language which often causes a surrounding silence to spread about it, and so it was with Chris Venner, that as he poured out the words in a low voice which was trembling and tense with emotion, Holden found it impossible to answer for the moment, but he looked down to the floor and then glanced around him. He saw the worn upholstery, its flowers more than half worn away, all the spring gone out of the roses, all the gold gone from the hearts of the daisies. He saw the carpet, polished and worn almost white along the seams; he saw the cracked windowpanes, one light entirely knocked out but filled in with oiled paper, which in turn had a hole punched through it; he saw a terrible old piano in the corner of the big living room, with the veneer lifting from the surface of the instrument, suggesting an interior condition which only the demons of discord could even faintly imagine. He saw the cracked and soiled ceiling from which half the plaster had fallen and exposed the bared slats and discolored mortar; he saw the reeling weakness of the chairs; he saw the spur scars along the mop board; he saw the spider webs in the upper corners. He heard the flies buzzing busily in the central stream of white-hot sunshine; and from the outside of the building he heard the chickens cawing and cackling drowsily, the shrill snarling of the swine, the low of a cow.

How could God have created so much horrible ugliness? And yet this man desired to live here—his heart was breaking at the thought of leaving it! No, hardly that. But the house was nothing to Chris Venner. Fill it from wall to wall and from ceiling to cell with noise and confusion and good cheer and food and voices of companions—this was all he asked. As for beauty or the lack of beauty, he had no eye for it. His soul was not tuned to that key! No, let the chickens cackle, let the pigs whine in the distance, and let the bull roar from the pasture. Their voices carried to the brain of Chris Venner the sweetest triumphs of music, singing one and all: "I belong to Chris Venner. My body is his. He may have me when he will. He may convert me into food. He may convert me into dollars. I am a living, breathing, audible part of his substance. I am almost part of his flesh already!"

Such was the message which each brought home to the big man, and young Tom Holden, watching and listening, saw and understood. Not that he had ever read any of this in a book, but pain opens in a sensitive mind many doors which are closed forever in the intelligence of most people. It opens many doors, or it closes them all! As for Holden, he could guess and feel with the instinctive adroitness of a helpless thing—an animal, say, or a child. But he could apply his man's intelligence to what his senses taught him and his instincts urged. So, now, it seemed to him that he had taken the entire truth about Chris Venner inside his being. He knew all about that big, handsome, burly ruffian and reformed crook. He had Chris Venner in the hollow of one of his weak hands!

It was enough to have made another man feel like singing a song of triumph. But that was not so with Holden. He felt, rather, a deeply ingrained sense of humility and of sorrow. How much Chris Venner had achieved; how much more, still, could he go on achieving! He could add great things to his community. He could be a force in the world, therefore. But what could he, what could Holden do? Here was this strong-handed robber turning honest citizen at a rate that dazzled and bewildered Holden. Here was a valley quintupled in productiveness, so much taken from the desert and given to society—enough to support half a dozen or a dozen whole families, eventually, and one of those families might bring into the world a genius. Who could say in how much the production of that genius and the million blessings he would give the world was not the direct result of the big strong hands and the stupid, restless brain of Chris Venner?

These were the gloomy reflections of Thomas Holden. And they all flooded through his brain in the mere half second or second of silence which elapsed after the last sound of the voice of Mr. Christopher Venner had died away. Certainly he spoke long before Chris had a chance to become embarrassed.

"I suppose that there's something in all this beside the valley and the ranch, Chris?"

"I dunno what you mean, partner?"

"There's somebody you don't wish to have her learn—"

"About what I've done?"

"That's it."

"You're right, Holden. You're always right. I ain't said a thing about a girl, but there's one messed up in this—all tangled up inside of my head, so's I can't never get rid of her, day or night. She sticks with me like a burr into the wool of a fool sheep. I can't get her out, Holden. I can't do it. And I don't want to! I want to keep her. I want to have her and keep her the rest of her days and mine. I want her to have the burying of me after my time's up. I want her to hear the drop of the dirt on my coffin and go home to comfort my kids. Y'understand me, partner? I want her for a wife. Julie's a good girl! Too good, I'm thinkin' half the time. Too good to stay with me a minute after she hears about what I've been and the things that I've done! What d'you say, Holden? What d'you think she'd do?"

Holden could barely repress a smile. It was a very like the

110

babbling of a child which cannot end talking until it has spilled out all of its soul which it can put into words. Such was this outburst of big Chris Venner.

"Does she love you?" asked Holden and as he used the word, he could not help wincing, for he thought of the bright, scornful eyes of the lady of his heart, fixed irremovably upon his soul, withering it like a blast of fire.

"Love," said Chris thoughtfully, "is something that I ain't been bothering with enough to know much about it at all. But she's got a way of lookin' sort of friendly at me. I feel as if I could talk to Julie about most things. I feel as if she'd even understand if I was to talk to her about herself. There's only one devil in it—what would happen if she was to find out—"

"About how you made your start?"

"Stolen money, Holden!"

"I understand. Well, there may be a way."

"If you find it," said Chris, a moisture of intense emotion springing into his eyes, "I tell you that I'll go to hell and back again for you, Holden."

"Suppose," said Holden, "that the bank was to forgive you and dismiss the search for the criminal and even send you a private vote of thanks?"

"Are you laughin' at me?" asked Chris sadly.

"I'm telling you exactly what may be done. The bank that you and Blinky Wickson touched up doesn't want vengeance. It wants hard cash—the same hard cash that was taken out by you and Blinky. If it had that money back, it would let vengeance go hang itself. Besides, it would consider you the closest thing to a saint and an honest man—perhaps those two words mean the same—that this century has given to the world."

"I'm tryin' to foller you," said Chris Venner.

"It's very simple. You and Blinky stole fifty-eight thousand dollars from that bank. You've invested that money and struck a gold mine. The money was only a part of it. The moment you went straight you stopped being a beggar and turned into a man of substance. Well, Chris, you now have a bank behind you that will back you to the limit. Thirty thousand is all that you need for yourself and your farm, irrigation section and all. And here's a bank which will let you have a hundred thousand and think nothing of it. Well, sir, doesn't it seem to you that you could afford to put aside sixty thousand and repay the very people that you and Blinky robbed? Principal and interest!"

Mr. Venner merely stared at him, for a moment, as the thought sank home in him.

"I'd never dare let 'em see me," he said, shaking his head. "They'd take back the money, and then they'd send me to prison. That's what'd happen."

"I'll manage that for you, Chris. The money will be restored to the bank. And there's an end of the matter. I'll take it with me and dispose of it for you so that the *whole* account against you will be closed. Unless you're afraid that I'd run away with your money and never bring it to the bank?"

Venner laid a hand on his arm. "You could run away with my right hand," he said solemnly. "*I'd* never put it against you, Holden. You could run away with dog-gone near everything I got. If it hadn't been for you, I'd of blowed in all I had playing cards, or followin' the ponies, or some fool thing like that, or else I'd have a knife in my gizzard and be lyin' out in the desert watchin' the buzzards drop out of the sky at me. But you made me go straight, old-timer. I tell you—I'd be scared to go crooked after talkin' to you!"

"If you've paid back the bank," said Holden, "your past is as clear as a slate. Everything that stands against you is rubbed out. Then, there's no tale that could ever be carried to Julie. Isn't that right?"

"Holden, you see right through everything to the bottom of it!"

"You'll take my advice?"

"Yes, and God bless you!"

"Go see your bank, then, Venner. When you have that money in hard cash, come back to me."

"Holden," said the big man, "what could I ever do for you?"

"Something I intend to ask of you later. I've come to get your help in something, Chris."

It was as though he had promised a great benefit to the rancher. Venner was as happy as a child. And afterward he took the cripple with him as he drove about his place and showed him the region which was to be irrigated.

"I was like that—dry ground when I met you," he said to Holden. "Dog-goned if you ain't reclaimed me. But what I want to know is, when you take that coin to the bank, how're you going to be sure that they won't have you pinched?"

"You must leave that to me," answered Holden, retiring behind his cloud of mystery.

Venner blinked at the sunburned hills; then he nodded in a mute admittance that there was much in his companion which he could never hope to fathom.

22

WHEN THEY CAME back to the old ranch house, they found a piebald mustang with thrown reins standing in front of the place, and at the sight, Venner so quickened the pace of the return that his companion was prepared for what he met. A tall girl with a brown face and a frizzing of weather-bleached hair beneath the brim of a man's hat—a long-striding, deep-voiced girl with a foot like a man's and a hand like a man's hand, and yet with something inevitably and delightfully feminine about her. There was no need to ask whether or not this were Julie Hendricks. Her smile and the glimmering of her eyes as she saw big Chris Venner were enough to announce it. And Holden saw Venner, as they went forward, quivering with delight.

They were introduced, and when he had bowed to Miss Hendricks and shaken her hand, he heard Venner repeating: "This is *the* Holden!"

"Oh," cried Julie, "I was blind! And I didn't remember. I've heard more about you than would fill a book smack up with fairy tales, Mr. Holden."

He found occasion to take the stallion to the stables immediately and left Chris and Julie together. When he came back, they were a little more flushed, a little more foolishly happy in expression. Before Julie rode away, again, she found a chance to speak to Holden alone.

"I dunno all that you've done for Chris. Of course he ain't much of a talker," said she. "But I know that he thinks that he owes everything to you. I guess you're the best friend that he has on earth. And, I hope that you'll be my friend, too, Mr. Holden!"

She said it with tears of sincerity in her eyes, as though she felt that his disapproval would be enough to drag big Chris Venner away from her. He put all her fears at rest at once.

"He doesn't need any help after this," said Holden, "except from you!"

So she went away, laughing and blushing, and Holden prepared for his own departure. He could not stay long on the ranch because, selfishly and to his great shame, the more he stayed there, the more he was annoyed by the happiness of Chris and the girl, and more keenly he felt that he himself was shut away from all such joys in life!

And there was, above all, the babble of Chris to trouble him, for now that he had seen the girl he had to give his opinion of her and admit that she was beautiful, brilliant, gentle, and wise. The next morning they went to the bank of Chris, and Venner came back to him after a long delay.

"They didn't want to do it. That much cash stripped them short, and it was only luck that they happened to have so much coin on hand. Credit is what they work by!"

But there he had it. Sixty thousand dollars in bills—a fine little fortune which, invested with any skill, would keep a man from want all of his days. Yet his fear was never for a moment that his friend might run away with the prize. All that he worried about was that trouble of some kind might come to Holden during this dangerous errand.

"They go hand in glove with detectives," said Venner. "I know all about that. They'd jail you quicker'n a wink if they got the chance, returned money or not. But, Holden, if you manage to do this for me, and hush up the thing forever, so's it'll never have a chance to come back at the ears of Julie— why, I'd die for you, Holden!"

"When I come back," answered Tom, "you may have your chance."

After that dark warning, he rode away. There was a nine hours' journey before him, even for the tireless speed of big Clancy. They had to climb out of the region of silver spruce and lofty pines to the levels of the lodge-pole pines, those vanguards of forest advances. They crossed a bleak range and dropped down into a bright, green-faced little valley where two slow streams flowed from north and south, met in a little lake, and then rolled westward, but in diminished masses, for the opening from the lake was dammed high, the lake itself much magnified, and the waters which were backed up served to water a quantity of otherwise useless desert.

But the desert was gone from that hollow. Where there had once been only a streaking of grass on either side of the rivers and where the willows on the banks were almost the only trees, half a dozen years of cultivation had flooded the whole valley with pleasant fields, and rich orchards of a paler green.

The air at the level of the height from which Holden looked down was crystal clear and his eye, at a single step, could leap across to the farther side of the valley. But beneath him the mists from the wet fields rose like smoke, thin, but in layer on layer, clouding the glass, as it were. And as the wind stirred strongly this delicate mist, he saw certain things by glimpses, such as the blinking windows of the neat little town in the center of the valley on the edge of the lake. That was his goal. Yonder was the Maybeck bank in the town of Maybeck; yonder was Julius Maybeck, whose frantic appeals to justice since his bank was robbed had made himself famous and laughed at through the cattle country. Even Holden, somber minded though he was, smiled as he started Clancy down the slope toward Maybeck.

Here was no crossroads village. When he entered it, the shod hoofs of Clancy rang upon bitumen pavements. There were gutters made of heavy stones, three feet long, looking as strong and as stubborn as iron. There were neat little houses, built after the fashion of California bungalows, each with a gaily painted roof, a deep veranda, and set back behind a lawn with a palm standing in it, or a great-armed cactus. And such was the cheerful face of the town of Maybeck! A town that had sprung up under the magic of one man's hand!

Holden, as he journeyed through it, took a careful note of the place. It was no wonder that the place had been able to withstand the loss of sixty thousand dollars, or thereabouts. Ten times that loss could not have ruined the town of Maybeck!

He reached the center of the town. It was a large square in the center of which stood the county courthouse made formidable as the seat of the county powers by a classic front of five columns built of granite courses and donated to the county by Mr. Julius Maybeck, himself, he for whom the

town and then the county had been named—the benefactor—
the farsighted banker who had founded the prosperity of the
whole valley!

And just as Mr. Holden saw the courthouse, someone saw
Mr. Holden. He was aware of a stir and a buzz of comment
in a group which stood in front of the cigar store. The
whisper ran out to the curb. Someone in an automobile
turned to stare.

They seemed both surprised and horrified. And Holden
himself was amazed. He knew that his reputation in Larramee
was most unsavory, but he was amazed to find that he was
known at such a distance from the latter town.

He went on, however, until he found the bank. There was
no mistaking it. It was like the courthouse, except that it was
smaller. That mysterious instinct in American businessmen
which makes them plant a bank that looks like a Greek
temple in the midst of skyscrapers of a downtown district,
made Mr. Julius Maybeck plant another bank in the guise of
a Greek temple among the little bungalows of the village.
Holden noted the solemn and classic face of the imposing
structure with a smile.

Then he left the stallion at the curb. There was no need to
tether him. He and Sneak had grown to be great companions,
and while the dog lay curled on the ground beneath his head,
no one would dare to approach the stallion, and Clancy, in
turn, would not leave the dog.

Half a dozen people gathered to watch him dismount, but
they gathered at a respectful distance, whispering to one
another. Certainly he was well known in Maybeck!

He entered the bank with his staff, and a moment later he
sat down in front of Julius Maybeck.

23

JULIUS MAYBECK was easily the most important man in the
valley. Everyone admitted his rating, and Mr. Maybeck was
the first one to discover his own significance. When the doctor

sent him West for a vacation, after his hard work in a New York haberdashery had broken down his nerves, Mr. Maybeck could not leave his business acumen behind him. And when he reached this valley, ostensibly for quiet and hunting, he spent his time, instead of carrying a gun, in staring down at the yellow waters of the little rivers, dreaming of dollars.

A year later his haberdashery was sold, and Mr. Maybeck was in the West at work on his scheme.

That was twelve years before. In the interval the dam had been financed, the valley cut up into ten- and twenty-acre farms, and the range land turned into a garden. All the profits did not go to the late haberdasher. He had not enough money to finance the scheme in its entirety. But he always felt that the others who had made money out of the scheme were his great debtors. They were grateful to him, but in the eyes of Mr. Maybeck, they were not grateful enough.

This thought of the ingratitude of the world kept a continual shadow on his brow and in his mind. And sometimes, when he thought of his own virtues and his own genius, so ill rewarded, tears flooded his eyes.

He had money, of course. He had plenty of money. But as he used to say: "Money ain't everything. There's something else!"

Exactly what he had in mind, no one ever knew, not even Mrs. Maybeck. But in reality Mr. Maybeck was dreaming of a day when the valley which had been named after him would awaken to his great services and, to perpetuate his fame, erect to him a statue in the central square of the town which his ability had conjured into existence. Not stone. Not even marble would do. It must be imperishable bronze, and on a pedestal, lettered in lasting iron, some such motto as this:

To Julius Overman Maybeck, philanthropist and financier, whose genius, whose generosity, and whose foresight created this city and all that is in it, erected by a grateful people, conscious of his virtues, that his name may be constantly before them and before their children.

Something like this would have been to the point. Not entirely enough, but still, a hint—a milestone pointing in the right way. And every time there was a meeting of the city's council, Mr. Maybeck in his heart of hearts wondered who would advance this worthy proposition.

No one did. Time rolled on. The years grew old. And this beautiful and appropriate action was not performed. There came a time when Julius Overman Maybeck began to feel that it would be necessary for him to plant the germ of the idea in some other mind, so that it might be proposed. And just as he was about to broach the subject to the mayor, who had recently benefited through a large loan from the bank, the blow fell, and the safe was opened, and nearly sixty thousand dollars was taken from the vault.

It was not the cash lost that hurt Mr. Maybeck. In the first place, only a portion of that loss came upon him, and that share of it which struck him, was but a scratch upon the fair face of his fortune. That was not the trouble. What grieved him to the heart was that there should have been such baseness in the world as to strike him—a benefactor of humanity—one who had helped to turn the desert green for the benefit of others! It was a blow from which he could not recover. From that day his face was black. The genial air left him. The kindness passed away from his business dealings.

"Business is business!" became the battle flag around which he rallied all the savage discontent that was in him.

And as he slapped his fat hand on the edge of his desk and leaned forward in his chair to stare at Mr. Holden, the "business is business" look was in his eyes.

"What is your name?" asked he.

"Holden," said the cripple.

At this, the man of money reached backward toward a bell in the wall behind him, and then checked himself mid-gesture, so to speak, and grew white and flabby of cheek as he glowered at the young man.

"You're Holden!" he said huskily, at last.

"Yes."

"Thomas Holden?"

"Yes."

"God have mercy on my wretched soul," sighed Julius Maybeck. "There is no justice in this world. Now *you* have come to pillage me and my bank?"

"In what way?" asked Holden curiously. "Here you are surrounded by your men. Here am I all alone."

"My men," sighed the banker, "work for the sake of small wages. Their souls are not in the business."

"Suppose," said Holden, "that I tell you I have come for quite another matter."

"Such as what, my friend?"

"To do you good, say?"

Mr. Maybeck smiled dryly. "Very likely," said he.

"You have heard a good deal about me, I presume?" said Holden.

"Here and there—we have picked up a good deal about your doings, Mr. Holden."

"And everything you have heard has not been, altogether, favorable?"

"Not altogether! No, I dare say that it has not!"

"I have had robberies and murders laid to my account?"

"Exactly."

"Very well, Mr. Maybeck, even assuming that I have done all of these things, I may still be capable of doing you good."

Mr. Maybeck made a wide gesture with both hands, and his meaning was obvious. He desired to have proof before he talked further.

"For instance," said Holden, "it might be to my interest to undo the damage which other people have done you."

"Ah?"

"For many good reasons."

"I am waiting to hear you, Mr. Holden."

"There may come a time in the life of the most lawless man, Mr. Maybeck, when he finds that he needs something more than money."

"And that?"

"Protection, let us say."

"From what?"

"The law, Mr. Maybeck!"

"I thank heaven," said the banker, "that the law has been my friend all the days of my life."

"I thank heaven," answered Holden, mimicking unconsciously the words and the tone of the other, "that the law has never laid a hand on me up to this time. But suppose that I wish to have some further resource? Suppose that I conceive of a time to come when I may need the help of honest people?"

"What could they do?"

"Speak for me when I am in trouble. Help me as if I am cornered by the same law that we have been speaking of, and perhaps, when the worst comes to the worst, hire a lawyer for me, promise him good pay, and see that he fights the case through."

"This is all very sensible," said the banker. "I suppose," he added, smiling grimly, "that I am your object in this?"

"I intend to buy your interest," said Holden.

"Ah?"

"Exactly that."

"There is no money—" began Maybeck, and then stopped and flushed.

"Which could hire your intercession for a criminal? You mean that?"

"I have not said it. But a banker has a certain position."

"Nevertheless, there is a price which may be reached for most men after which they become interested in whatever is said. I think that I may interest you, Mr. Maybeck."

One might have expected the honest Mr. Maybeck to flush with rage at such a suggestion as this, but the honest Mr. Maybeck was not at all enraged. He was too curious. And though he heard a man declare that he believed the banker was capable of taking a bribe, Mr. Maybeck merely shrugged his shoulders and prepared to listen. He considered his virtue so strong that the idea of a fall from glory was ridiculous to him.

"Very well," said he.

It was as though he had said: "Begin, tempter!"

"I am dealing in large figures from the start," said Holden, "because I want large support from an important man. A man like you, Maybeck, can elect members to the State senate and assembly merely by speaking a word. A man like you has a distinct and a direct weight with the governor."

Mr. Maybeck cleared his throat. This was not altogether unpleasing. He began to see that Holden was something more than a criminal. He was a brilliant mind capable of great insight.

"These things are possible, perhaps," said he.

"Ten thousand dollars is my retainer's fee to you, for your good influence in case I get into trouble," said Holden.

The banker's flush grew brighter. It was a large sum of money. Ten thousand dollars in cash would build the whole new wing to his house which he had planned, and enlarge his stable also. Ten thousand was a year's salary for an important man. Ten thousand, by its very mention, made him look toward Mr. Holden in a new manner. He ceased to be a mere robber. Robbery became a business, considered in the light of such finance, and Holden was a businessman—following a lucrative business, at that.

Still, ten thousand was not enough. The mention of such a sum merely served to make him more acutely aware of his own virtue. He flushed warmly; a delicious sensation of joy ran through his flesh.

"I feel that you are a man of discretion, Holden," said he. "And I appreciate what you have to say. Nevertheless—I tell you frankly and truthfully—that I cannot be bought. My influence, such as it is, cannot be exchanged for dollars!" He sat back in his chair and shook his head.

He added: "Ten thousand is a large sum. Apply it to a good purpose—"

"Ten thousand?" said Holden calmly. "You misunderstood. Twenty thousand was the amount I mentioned."

Mr. Maybeck stopped wagging his head. He stared fixedly at his companion, and as he stared, he saw another vision, great and bright and terrible. He saw the dreadful picture of himself submitting to the temptation and accepting the bribe.

Then he rolled out of his chair, pitched to his feet, and began to pad hastily up and down the linoleum of his office on his rubber heels, glancing out the clouded glass which walled him in and which nevertheless gave him sight of the shadowy line at the paying teller's window and the shadow of the paying teller himself behind the barred window.

It was the horror of fear of yielding that checked him.

"Mr. Holden," said he, "you talk to me like a man who had no conscience—" Then he added hastily, remembering that this visitor most probably carried a gun and knew how to use it— "I mean to say, money cannot move me. I know myself. I know money. Money cannot budge me. Go somewhere else. Offer them your money. But with me—" He shook his head and sighed. "It won't do, Mr. Holden! It won't do!"

"Very well," said Holden. "I am the last man in the world to offer a bribe. Consider, rather, that I am simply opening up business relations with you?"

"Eh?" gasped out the banker, grasping at the thought and then failing to seize it firmly enough.

"I said," went on Holden, "that I would consider a sum of thirty thousand dollars—"

"Did you say thirty thousand?" asked Maybeck softly.

"I said thirty or forty thousand," answered Holden firmly. "Didn't you hear me?"

"I suppose that I did."

"I said that I would consider thirty or forty thousand dollars well invested."

"To buy me!" cried the banker wringing his hands. "To buy my soul. Oh, heaven defend me!"

"Nonsense," answered Holden, feeling a sort of fierce joy as he saw that weak and flabby soul melting under the fire. "Nonsense, man! It is merely as I would pay a lawyer a retaining fee. I am trying to buy his interest—not his honesty! Buy you? Why, Mr. Maybeck, the whole world knows that you're worth a million if you're worth a penny!"

He had trebled the actual fortune of the banker, but Maybeck nodded. The belief in strength is sometimes strength.

"How could I buy you," said Holden, "with a mere forty or fifty thousand dollars?"

Here the banker came stiffly erect.

"Did you say fifty thousand dollars?" he asked huskily.

"I said fifty thousand dollars," said Holden, "not for your direct interest in my affairs, but your influence with the judge who may some day try me. For your influence with the governor for a pardon in case I am one day sentenced. For these things, I would offer to you—as to a lawyer, do you understand? Or to an insurance company—fifty thousand dollars!"

"Bribery!" moaned the miserable Maybeck.

"Is law a dishonest or a dishonorable business?"

"God forbid!"

"Is insurance illegal?"

"No, no!"

"Very well, sir! What is your answer?"

"My head is spinning," said the banker. "I try to see both sides of this question. Surely, surely there are two sides. I have seen dishonesty in honest people. Surely there may be honor in a—"

122

"In a thief? Perhaps there is. It is a possibility, at least. I have heard about it in books. And for sixty thousand dollars—"

"Sixty thousand?" echoed the poor banker.

"Exactly."

"Man, man, can you be sure of yourself when you speak of such a vast sum?"

"You understand, sir? With this money you can replace what was taken from your bank."

"By the eternal gods!" cried Maybeck. "You are the man who plundered the bank!"

He looked at Holden as at a midday ghost. Holden had hardly expected to have the matter take this turn. However, he was suspected of so much already that it was impossible to be more under the shadow.

"I have asked you a question," said Holden. "Sixty thousand, Mr. Maybeck?"

"Enough," said the poor banker. "But about the money—"

"I have your word?"

"Yes, yes, yes."

"Shake hands with me."

"Very well, Holden. I wish you luck."

"But will you work to give me luck?"

"Why not? Why not?"

"If you should fail, I would find a way to pass the word to my friends. Do you know what they would do, Maybeck?"

"Eh?"

"They would cut your throat, my fat friend, from ear to ear!"

"Phaugh! Well, well, Holden. We have shaken hands on the thing. And now—the money? You said sixty thousand?"

He was nodding and trembling with delight and with avarice.

"Here," said Holden, "is the money."

He drew out a packet, an astonishingly little packet. And he placed it on the desk. The banker tore the package open and examined the bills feverishly.

"It is not the same," he said with a sigh. "It is not the same money which was taken from our vaults. However, it is the will of God. He took away and He returned it again. Mysteriously, but truly."

"I, then," said Holden sneeringly, "am able to consider myself an agent of God?"

"You?" cried the other. "No, no! You are the devil himself!" He added, gripping the arm of Holden. "But even if you are the devil, you will find it hard to get out of this trouble, Holden. Look!"

He swept his arm toward the glass walls, and Holden saw all around him a thickly pressed line of men, their dim shadows falling on the clouded glass.

"They are waiting," said the president, "for my signal!"

"Your signal?"

"Do you think that we are fools in this town of Maybeck? I tell you, Holden, that the moment you entered the bank a clerk telephoned to me."

"And told you that I had come?"

"Exactly!"

"And what of that?"

"What of that? Man, man, you don't know that everything is known! We understand. The story was spread all through the mountain towns early this morning by the telegraph, and they have put out a reward for you that will bring out a thousand armed men hunting for you before noon!"

Holden grew sick and pale. "What have they charged against me?" he asked.

"That you murdered—a devilish thing to have done, man— that you murdered in cold blood old Alec Marshall and his son, at Timber Valley!"

"I murdered two men?"

"Holden, they have the proofs. A man on a red horse, the color and the size of your stallion, was seen to leave Timber Valley. His trail was followed up the valley. There lay Alec and his boy dead in their shack. Holden, nothing can save you!"

"And when I entered the bank?"

"God forgive me, Holden, I had them send for the sheriff to take charge."

"Those are his men, then?"

"Those are his men!"

Holden sat down in a chair and took out a cigarette.

"What will you do?" breathed the banker.

"Smoke," said Holden, "and think the thing over!"

24

THE SHERIFF was a man who was worthy of his place. He was no politician who had gained office through shaking hands and telling stories and laughing at the poor wit of every man of the street. He was a fighter. In the far mountains he had spent an apprenticeship of twenty years catching animals in traps and still hunting them with guns. From this he graduated to the more exciting business of hunting men.

He worked for the love of the work. He hated a criminal as much as he hated a "varmint." Cowardly and cruel as a wolf or a coyote might be, it was the opinion of the sheriff that the cruelty and the cowardice of a criminal was apt to exceed by far all the wickedness of any animal. Therefore he hunted them down religiously and remorselessly.

He had held office for only two terms. When he came, he found Maybeck County with its newly found prosperity, a hunting ground for crooks of all descriptions. But during the last two years the only crime worth calling a crime that had taken place in the county, had taken place in the robbery of the bank itself. Such had been the efficiency of his labors!

When he got the telephone message from the bank that the much-heralded Holden was in that building, he did not wait for his deputy, who had gone around the corner for tobacco. He started out as he was. He did not even go into the back room for his hat. His long, tangled locks in themselves must protect his head and shade his eyes.

On the way he picked up what assistance he wanted. He

125

signaled his assistants one by one, a man here and a man there—all trained and proven fighters. Better three good men than thirty "talkers," as the sheriff was apt to call the heroes of the hotel stove side.

He had more than three good men with him when he reached the bank, however. He had been peculiarly lucky as he went down the main street of the town. At one swoop he had gathered in the three Morrissey brothers, each as good a man as the other, and every one a crack shot and a fighter who would fight for the love of the battle and for no other inducement.

The sheriff reached the bank, therefore, in high fettle. He had behind him no fewer than eleven hard-headed, hard-handed, strong-riding, straight-shooting heroes. Perhaps some men of the law would have scorned such reinforcements. They would have gone to make the arrest themselves, single-handed. But the sheriff did not care in the least about show. He had been a trapper. And trappers do not care about the beauty of the beast, the courage of his last stand, the loveliness of the deer in flight, the puma at bay. What he wants is pelts and bounties. And he gets them, though not in showy ways. This man of the law had no fear. But he had no folly, either. He never boasted, and he never threw away a chance. He could make himself striking and popular through his record, and through his record only. Even those who knew him best were apt to be those who feared him most, for the more he knew of human nature, the more he declared the seeds of the devil were in all of us! That was certain.

This was the leader of the thick line of broad-shouldered men who surrounded the office of the president and whose shadows fell inward upon the walls of clouded glass. And as they gathered there, they turned to the sheriff for orders.

"Shall we bust in?" their eyes asked him.

He shook his head. They asked him again, in words, after a time. Then he took the cashier aside.

"Is that office sound?" he asked.

"It's got glass walls," said the cashier.

"They's other kind of walls around the glass," said the sheriff, smiling toward those waiting guards of his. "What about the ceiling and the floor?"

"The ceiling is eleven feet from the floor. It's hard, thick plaster under steel lath—and—"

"That's enough," said the sheriff, "because he ain't gonna melt his way through that, I guess. Now what about the floor?"

"Flags laid across boards—"

The sheriff raised his hand and smiled. Then he went back to the line and said calmly: "Boys, there's no use hurryin' that trap. Let it make its own catch. They're still talkin'. And when the president is ready for us to work, he'll be ready to stop talkin'. We've got him caught. I guess he's worth waitin' for. Speakin' personal, I'd as soon wait all day for the sight of this here Holden behind the bars."

The others nodded. The sheriff had won too many times for them to doubt him now.

In the meantime, though it seemed a foolish precaution, he guarded against the possible retreat of the criminal. Yonder in the street stood the great red-bay stallion, Clancy, and under the head of the big horse lay the shaggy wolf dog, Sneak. Admittedly, once the cripple sat on the back of Clancy, it was sheerest folly to pursue him. The thing to do was to keep him from getting at the horse.

So the sheriff went out and posted his deputy, who had come to the scene by this time with a full half dozen well-armed men who had also gathered, around Clancy and the big dog. It might have seemed a great deal more than was necessary, this flock of men, this little army. But as has been said before, the sheriff was not a man who ever threw away a single chance. He made his victories count by their completeness, not by their glory.

If he could get five men to fight against one, he would think it sheerest madness to go into the battle with mere odds of three to one.

Then he returned to the line which waited around the president's office. It was now pointed out to the sheriff that for ten minutes there had been no sound of voices from the office, coming dimly and muffled through the heavy glass and wood walls of the room.

Still he was in no hurry. "Maybe they're talkin' soft," he said.

But the word passed out into the street that probably the capture would be made by forcing the office door at any minute. And people began to brace their nerves to prepare for the shock of the explosions of guns. Because it was taken for granted that so terrible a person as the famous and mysterious little cripple would never let himself be taken except at an awful price.

The whole town of Maybeck was there—hundreds and hundreds of people packed in around the front of the bank. And then a sharp, thin whistle cut the air from a distance a block away down the street. It was a most ordinary sound, but it made the great stallion prick his ears and toss up his head. And the guards stood closer in a ring around him, facing resolutely any attack. The attack came, but not from the expected quarter. It came from the rear, the stallion himself rushing suddenly forward. He knocked down five men in the crowd in the first leap. The wolf dog slashed the bodies of three more. Then yells of "Mad dog!" scattered the throng and left a broadening path down which the red horse and the gray dog streaked.

They whipped around the first corner. Then the hoofbeats stopped suddenly; and every one in the crowd knew why the horse had paused. By a miracle, Holden was there!

25

A LITTLE CHILD, himself a cripple so that he had been delayed far behind the other children when the rumor swept them toward the center of the town and the bank itself, was the only one to see the actual details of how the wolf dog and the great red horse came storming around the corner of the street up to the little man who waited for them, covered with dust, his clothes torn, looking as though he had been trampled in the dust by a wild herd. He saw the stallion pause. He saw the cripple clamber to the saddle with infinite pains, his face contorted with the agony of his haste and of his effort. He saw the man loosen the reins. He saw the great horse dart away down the street just as the far-flung foreguard of the sheriff's men came whirling around the corner in their pursuit. They had time to pour in one crashing, rattling volley as the red stallion swung out of view. And that was the last they saw of Clancy or Clancy's rider on that day.

By the time they reached the edge of the town, no matter how fiercely they spurred, Clancy had swept his rider away into the concealment of the hills; and after that they could never sight him. In the meantime, the sheriff and those who were nearest about him standing near the office of the president of the bank, when they heard from the street the wild shout that the criminal was escaping, waited no longer, but half a dozen stout shoulders were leaned against the door and burst it open. They lurched into the office and there they were able at a glance to see the cause of escape. For Mr. Maybeck lay stretched upon the floor, and he was swathed head and foot in thickly twisted ropes. A handkerchief, wadded into his throat, prevented him from making any outcry, and his face was swollen and purple, his eyes starting from his head from the violence of his exertions to work the gag from between his teeth with his tongue.

Beside the excellent Julius Maybeck, that benefactor of the city, there were heaps of bricks which had been worked out of the floor, and it was plain from the worn and even bleeding fingers of Mr. Maybeck that he had been forced to join the robber in the work of tearing up the flooring. Perhaps under the point of that villain's gun he had been compelled to labor and at the same time to keep up that noisy conversation which was constantly audible to those outside the chamber as a confused blur of sound. No doubt it had been confused indeed in every fact, had they been able to make out the words which were obscurely jumbled together.

The bricks had been lifted from a considerable hole; beneath that circumference the boards had been cut through or pried up, and in this fashion Mr. Thomas Holden had gained access to the cellar of the bank after first binding and gagging the president of the institution so that there was nothing to fear from any alarm which he might raise.

In the meantime, Thomas Holden was gone; and the men of Maybeck felt that they had joined the great company of those whom the resolute villain had made ridiculous.

They were doing their best to circulate among the hills and come upon some traces of the direction of his flight; while he, at that moment, sat his horse under the window of big Chris Venner in the dusk of the evening.

"Chris," he said, "everything is settled. Old Maybeck is certain that I stole the money and now I have given it back to him to buy his good influence. And so, Chris, no human being can ever bring the shadow of that theft against you so long as you live."

"You've taken it on yourself, Holden?" murmured Venner. "Can I stand for that?"

"They've chalked up murder against me now," said Holden. "A little thing like stealing really doesn't matter. Now, Chris, I've come to tell you what you can do for me to pay back everything."

"Old-timer, I been waitin' to hear you talk."

"They've accused me of murdering old Alec Marshall and his son in Timber Valley. Chris, do you know that country?"

"I know it, and I know everybody in it."

"Do you know the crooks who hang around there?"

"I learned the game while I was there, man!"

"Go up to Timber Valley, Chris. As sure as there's a God in heaven, the same devil who murdered Alec Marshall is the same devil who had been killing and robbing near Larramee, the one whose work they've charged up to me. Chris, you have to find that man and you have to turn him over to me."

"I?"

"You can do it, I think. I've worked out a plan."

"Look here, Holden, that fellow, if he ain't you—is the—"

"Listen to me, Chris, no matter what I've done in my life, I've never murdered in cold blood." He could have laughed aloud at the mere thought. He who had never had it in his power to injure anything, man or beast, that had power enough to stand and fight, or speed enough to turn and run. And yet here was big Chris Venner grown pale and troubled, and studying him out of frowning eyes.

"By heavens, Chris," Holden said, "you have believed all of these things that the idiots have been saying about me. Is that right?"

"I don't know. I don't know that I understand what—"

"Hush, Chris. Believe me when I tell you that I am not a devil and that I'm not a man eater."

Venner smiled faintly. It was very plain that his doubts concerning his companion were most grave.

"In one word," said Holden, "I shall show you that there is

130

another who had done all of the things—all of them—that have been charged against me around the town of Larramee."

"I'll be the gladdest man in the world when that's done, partner."

"I am the baited trap, Chris," said the cripple. "You are the trapper. And the fur-bearing animal that we want is the cur who has been raving through the night like a mad dog without a bark—full of poison and silence."

"I'm tryin' real patient to foller what you mean, Holden."

"It is this. I start for the mountains now. I aim for old Sugar Loaf there in the north. I travel very slowly. In the morning you announce that you were held up by Tom Holden and that I took sixty thousand dollars in hard cash away from you. You understand?"

"Suppose that I say that—what of old Maybeck? He'll start talkin' about the sixty thousand that he got; pretty soon, I'll get connected up with him and then—the whole dog-gone yarn will spill out!"

"Not a bit. I've bought Maybeck and tied up his mouth with money. He won't dare to talk about anything. I bought his soul, Chris. The fat-faced idiot would risk his right arm to help me or to do what I ask him to do in any respect. Very well, tomorrow morning you will start in for town and on the way through you'll lodge a complaint. You understand? Everybody must hear you! You'll talk loud and you'll talk long about the inefficiency of the law, about the way in which the sheriff of the counties and of the State allow criminals to override the entire country. You'll demand a change and swear that the country has become impossible to live in. You'll talk of sixty thousand dollars. You'll talk of ruin. You'll make it as black as possible!"

"Well?" asked Venner. "Tell me how that gives me a chance to help you to catch the gent that's been doin' the murderin'?"

"I'll explain that very quickly. The moment you are convinced that the entire town feels you have actually lost sixty thousand dollars, you must head back from the town and go straight to your own house. There you must pick up my trail."

"For the Sugar Loaf?"

"Yes. It will be marked so clearly that a child could read it. I'll leave an unmistakable trail, my friend. Follow along until the evening. By that time when the sun goes down, you can be sure that you will be within striking distance, for I intend to pick out a spot to camp in the middle of the afternoon and to remain there, preparing a comfortable camp. So, when you get toward the sunset time, you must be very cautious. I shall try to find a place in a hollow. In the center of some big clearing, with the trees all around the edge of it, I'll build my fire.

"Now, Venner, you must start stalking that fire. But the game you will be looking for will not be for me, but for the murderer!"

"What?"

"The murderer will be there, on the edge of that same clearing."

"My heavens, Holden!" breathed the big man.

He had changed color. Every whit of blood was gone from his face.

The explanation was simple enough, from the viewpoint of Holden. Having it noised abroad that sixty thousand dollars had been stolen from big Venner, that rumor, traveling with the usual speed of bad news, would be sure to reach the hearing of the archcriminal whose robberies and whose killings had reached such awful proportions near Larramee, and whose crimes had been saddled upon Holden's own shoulders. When the tidings reached the ears of that devil incarnate, he was sure to go to the house of Venner for the sake of picking up the trail of the successful reported robber.

Once on that trail, he would find his work very easy—made easy on purpose by the false-fugitive Holden himself, who would break off twigs, and ride through spots of soft dirt, and leave fallen cigarettes in the way, until the murderer, whoever he might be, was close to the camp which Holden would pitch in some readily accessible place.

But he would not act in the daytime. Everything went to prove that the destroyer loved the darkness of the night. All of his crimes had been committed at that hour. All of his successful robberies had been the fruit of the hours of dusk or full night. Therefore, no matter how near he came to Holden, the probability was that he would wait before he struck at his prey.

In the meantime, according to the directions which Holden left behind him, big Chris Venner, secret, swift, and strong, would be following along the same trail, looking for the hunter. And there was at least one chance in two that, while the murderer lurked in the brush, Chris Venner might come upon him and strike him down, as he had struck down Blinky Wickson.

All of this reasoning was clear enough to him. But big Venner, who naturally could not follow all of these mental processes off hand and who was inclined, from past experience, to attribute to Holden a sort of divine and mysterious foreknowledge and power of miraculous action, merely gaped at little Tom Holden, who was regarding him calmly from behind his glasses.

"What will the murderer be doin' there?" asked Venner.

"He'll be trying to murder me, Chris."

Venner moaned. "And you'll be sittin' there in a clearin' waitin' for him to do it?"

"He won't succeed, Chris. Take my word for that."

"Mr. Holden, I've heard you talk before—"

"One moment, Chris. Have you ever known me to be wrong?"

"Only—"

"And you think that I'd endanger my own life, Chris?"

Venner was half convinced by that blow. He drew in a long breath and regarded his smaller companion with unspeakable awe.

"Partner," he said, "it ain't no use for me to even try to understand you. You're too deep. You're a whole pile too deep!"

"One thing more," said Holden. "After you and I have caught the crook, you drop out of the picture."

"Eh?"

"I don't like to ask it, Chris. But after you've done that, you deny all knowledge of the thing. I want it to appear as my work and as my work only!"

Venner nodded, "The devil, man," said he modestly, "don't I know that you could do this all by yourself, and handle this here crook and me, too, all at the same time if you wanted to? Why, partner, you ain't doin' any more than tryin' me out with this. I'll show you that I'll do my job right."

"One thing more. Before you go, see Julie and tell her everything."

"Holden!"

"Tell her everything that ever happened in your life."

"D'you want to ruin me?"

"Take my advice. That's all I'll say!"

26

So ENDED WHAT was to big Chris Venner the strangest talk in his life. Afterward he pondered upon the matter carefully, solemnly, his chin in his hand, his brow knit.

It was not that he believed that the little man could be right. But it was because he felt in young Tom Holden the presence of a power of brains which he himself could never aspire toward. This controlling mystery he decided must be followed. He was told by the oracle to go to the lady and to confess. And as a pagan would obey a voice from the clouds, so he, with dread, against his will, against his reason, mounted his horse and rode to the house of handsome Julie Hendricks.

It was late. There was only one light burning in the house. And when he went around to it, there he found Julie in the kitchen, pressing a dress, working happily, busily over it, the heat from the work and the stove making her face rosy. He admired for some time the plumpness of her arm and the supple smoothness with which her wrist worked the heavy iron back and forth. What a wife she would be!

So he tapped at the back door, and when she opened it, he did not go inside, but took off his hat, and dropped it on the ground beside him, and held both her hands, and told her everything from the beginning, talking straight, talking fast, speaking through his teeth as though to an enemy, and then feeling her begin to tremble, and cursing Tom Holden for ever giving him any such advice as this had been.

But when he was ended, she dropped into his arms and wept. Not with sorrow and despair, but with utter joy.

Then, at last, she told him that rumors and that whispers came up to her from time to time. Too much was known about his past for her to remain in utter ignorance of the truth that he had been a wild young fool in his time. That wildness she could forgive, but not the concealment of it from herself.

An hour later, big Chris Venner rode slowly home through the evening with a chastened heart and a mind in which there were two conflicting ideas. The first was an all-possessing love for Julie, the tender and the true. The second was an equally deep awe for the wisdom of little Tom Holden, to which all the hidden things of the world and of the hearts of men and of women were revealed.

There was only one remaining mystery, and that was why such a man as he could ever need the help of a miserable, stupid creature such as Chris Venner.

So pondered Christopher. But, in the deep gratitude of his heart, he swore to himself that he would work for Holden the rest of his life, and particularly in this one affair, so that the little man could know that there was as much loyalty in him as there was generosity in Tom Holden himself.

Such were the thoughts of Chris Venner as he jogged back to his house. And in the meantime, the mysterious hero of his dreams, riding in another direction across the hills, found himself drifting, out of the sheerest loneliness to the house where his mother lived with the brawny brute called Cousin Joe Curtis, and his wolfish son, Gus.

For he had never felt so alone in the world. He had before him the dimmest of dim hopes, based upon the most intangible of intangible ideas. If he caught the murderer, by that prize he would have gained for himself two things. The first was the freedom from any actual criminal charge, no matter how thick suspicion might still be against him. The second and, in his eyes the greatest, was the opportunity to be near lovely Alexa Larramee, even for one evening of his life, though he might never see her again.

And yet all of these hopes were very cold, very small, as the night closed more thickly around him. His crippled leg grew numb with the pain of utter weariness. His heart was

135

sore. And he would have thrown away his life for the sake of a single moment of full-hearted joy.

But there was no joy in the world. Only two sparks hovered with him along the way, like fireflies in the world of blackness —Clancy and Sneak—Sneak like a dim gray ghost running before, and Clancy beneath him, resolutely stepping away through the night. They were a consolation. Without them he felt as though he would die.

It was the sheerest instinct which guided him, and no definite thought or volition. He rode down the trail into the upper valley without thinking where it might lead him.

He rode out of the upper valley into the foothills only vaguely aware that there was a sense of familiar things about him. And so, on a sudden, like a miracle rising before his eyes, he found himself in front of the house of Joe Curtis, with the light in the kitchen telling where his poor mother was slaving.

He left the red stallion in the dark among the trees before the house. He had hardly dismounted before Doc, the cur dog, came scurrying, whining with fury and with curiosity to bark at the strangers, as all cur dogs from the beginning of time have longed to do. But Doc was running upon his fate. As he neared the trees, a dim gray shadow hopped forth to meet him in one long bound. There was a flash and a click of teeth. Poor Doc, his throat torn wide, made not a sound. He turned to flee back to the house, and died after a few staggering steps.

Above him stood Holden and wondered over the poor brute. He was filled with pity. He was filled with a strange sadness such as he had never felt before. But he was also cold and strong with a new knowledge. For he could remember a time when old Doc had been the only friend of Tom Holden. In those old days the dog had seemed brave enough and strong enough to suit him—to be even quite a hero in the eyes of that other Tom Holden. That Tom Holden had wakened in the morning to wonder what new pain, what new humiliation the day would bring him to.

But here was a new man with new friends. Here was the red shadow of Clancy among the trees. What other horse was there in all the world to match with Clancy, and where was there another man to ride the great stallion? And here was Doc slain by the teeth of his other servant, his new dog, Sneak. It was significant of the new soul which inhabited the body of the cripple.

He took the glasses from his nose and dropped them into his pocket. Here in the dark, where no one could see him, there was no need for him to keep up that foolish farce.

He went to the kitchen window first. There he saw her at once. She had not changed an iota, except for a little deepening of the shadow of sadness which was upon her face.

She was as old, she was as bent, she was as patient. And in her face there was that beautiful resignation which, in other days, had seemed so detestable to him. He could understand it now. She had always bowed to the will of others—to the will of the men who were about her. She was a soldier obeying an officer. She was a slave obeying a master. And there was never a thought of revolt in her gentle eyes.

She had courage, too. She had will power. She had been able to educate him and make him fine and gentle in a way that no other man of the family had ever been. That was all her work. He could see, as he looked back now, how she had done it by long hours of the most loving and patient work. All of that had escaped him then. Because she had not known about the very books she urged him toward, he had despised her. Now he wanted to fall on his knees and kiss her hands.

She was making bread for tomorrow, greasing the tins, testing the heat of the ovens, putting in the fresh loaves. They would bake on and on until late in the night. Once he remembered, when he asked her if she did not dread baking nights and its long vigils, that she had answered that she loved it better than anything in the week. Because on other nights she had to go to bed early. But on this night she could stay up late and think her own thoughts.

That pure soul, that worn and tortured body! He marveled over her with tears; he saw her for the first time.

Then he went to the windows which looked in on the living room. Both Cousin Joe and his son were there, Joe looking as huge as ever, and Gus as long, as lean, as wolfish. And he had the same old and well-remembered habit of smiling silently to himself, his eyes secretly upon the floor, his long fingers caressing his mouth, his chin.

Cousin Joe seemed less monstrous than in the old times. But Gus seemed a little more awful than ever.

"Are you goin' out?" Joe was saying.

"I dunno. I guess so."

"Have you got plans?"

"Maybe."

"You don't do much talkin' these days, Gus?"

"What the devil good is it to talk to you, you old sap!" snarled out Gus.

He got up from his chair, yanked his hat deep over his eyes, and went to the door. There he stole a look back at his father, who had not moved from his place in front of the fire. And the upper lips of Gus curled away from his teeth more wolfishly than ever, so that the breath of the watcher in the night was taken.

After Gus went out and stamped down the board walk toward the horse corral, Holden still remained for a moment watching the form of the big man seated before the fire. He could not get over the marvel of it.

For, in another time, Gus would far rather have leaped into naked flames than to have encountered the wrath of his father by so much as an insolent glance. But here was rebellious talk, insolent talk, such talk as a man would not give to a dog. And yet big, proud fierce Joe Curtis endured it!

How could this thing be explained?

He went back to the kitchen window again. But he did not look in. Another thought had come over him. What would Miss Alexa Larramee, she of the millions, she of the proud friends, think when she came face to face with Mrs. Holden, if that day should ever come.

This was a whip stroke of exquisite torment. It made him flinch away into the darkness.

What would she think? How would she smile? If she smiled, he would hate her forever.

But how would he feel toward his mother?

He climbed up the lofty side of Clancy and rode away.

27

WHAT HOLDEN wanted, he found, exactly to his taste. It was a wide hill shoulder, flat-topped, without a tree upon it, though with a great skirting of giant pines at the edges of the open space. In the center of the open space, among a scattering of boulders of various sizes, he built his fire and cooked his supper. Then he turned Clancy forth to graze. And he patted the big stallion and used him tenderly; for who could tell whether or not he would ever mount the beautiful red body again?

As for Sneak, he had left the great gray dog behind him. On this occasion, it was his cue to be absolutely unprotected —to invite the blow, as it were. And such a creature of lightning suspicions and stealthy foot as Sneak was more apt by far to hunt than to be hunted.

But here was Holden in the trap, exactly as he had foreseen, with the chances some two in twenty that he would ever come out of the trap alive. For, after big Chris Venner scattered the tidings of the false theft through the town that day, there could be no doubt but that Mr. Murderer and Robber of Larramee would swiftly take horse for the trail of the pseudo-plunderer.

The late afternoon wore to the sunset. Holden put his back to a rock and faced the color in the west, calmly. And he heard varying sounds out of the big trees, but chiefly the triumphant singing of a squirrel in the top of a sapling. The little fellow clutched the very topmost twig of the lithe young

139

tree, which doubled over under the burden of his weight. There he swayed back and forth, tilted by a slight breeze, and chattered and raged his joy and his defiance to the world, and flaunted his plumy tail above his back. Holden picked up a pebble and flung it at the little gray braggart. It whirred sufficiently close to the target to make the squirrel utter one last bark of rage and scorn before it launched itself into the air. Down it sailed with the great tail spread out behind it, like a man under a parachute, gliding. It fell fast toward the ground at first, as Holden noticed, but then it seemed to flatten the arc of the fall and swooped off into the branches of a neighboring monster among which it instantly disappeared.

When Holden looked up from this event he found that the night was already closing fast over the hollow. The upper sky was still bright. The smoke from his camp fire, which was dying to red embers, passed upward invisible among the shadows of the trees, but when it reached the clearer region above, it was plainly to be seen, rising and melting like a ghost, until the sightless hand of the wind struck it, from time to time, and banished it to nothingness.

He was in the bottom of a great black well, he felt at times, looking up to a distant heaven. At last the color began to be smoked over by night; and at the same time the stars grew into the sky—little yellow points of flame.

Here was night upon him, and somewhere among the brush, somewhere in one of those twenty black-mouthed gaps in the trees, lurked the slayer, greedy for the gain which he foresaw, cruel-eyed, stealthy, already gripping his gun. And somewhere behind the killer, perhaps at that instant stealing near to him, was big Chris Venner, hunting the hunter.

Holden marveled at himself. For he had no fear. He searched through the soul which swelled and grew great in his starved body. No, there was no fear in him. He stood up and looked calmly around him. Yet he knew, in that time, that if he had had anything to which he could look and cling with any hope, he should have been filled with coldest terror. But there was nothing before him. It seemed to him that his life revolved around the thought of Alexa; and since the last hope of her was removed, he might as well end his existence. It was a dark blank before him.

He turned his back upon the black woods. And stepping to the fire he threw upon it half a dozen dry branches which he had prepared. Here was the light to brighten the target if the murderer wished to kill. Here was something which he could not fail to see. The branches crackled, the flames gathered noisily, and then leaped up through the topmost twigs with a loud rush. At once the arena bounded by the pines was illumined. Every face of every tree glistened in the burst of radiance, and yonder on the ground a skulking figure of a man rose to his knees and pitched a rifle to his shoulder.

The mind of Holden moved like the lightning flash. It seemed to him, so smoothly and precisely was he thinking, that he could draw his revolver and kill that fellow even before the gun exploded. Then he saw, at the same instant, another phenomenon behind the first form. Behind the first man a bulky form rose, and his shadow leaped up behind him across the trees. He descended like a huge beast of prey. He struck the rifleman and, as the gun exploded, the murderer was crushed to the ground.

As for the bullet, it sang wickedly near to the ear of Holden, but since it had missed, he waved the thought of it away. He was more interested in a brief struggle which occurred in the dark, two men whirling around and around. Neither, it seemed, had any advantage.

So Holden drew his revolver and advanced. He found them knitted together, writhing, gasping, feeling for a finishing hold. So he kneeled and thrust the muzzle of the gun under the chin of Venner's opponent.

There was a snarl of venom from the other. Then he relaxed his body in a token of surrender.

"Take him in to the fire," said Holden, and pushed himself up to his feet by the use of his staff.

In the inner circle, among the boulders, he turned and watched the killer, bundled before Venner, who kept a grip on one of the villain's arms, twisted behind his back, and had the mouth of a revolver pressed into the small of the man's back.

So they came into the bright neighborhood of the fire and Holden, with an exclamation, recognized Gus Curtis. And Gus, with a snarl, faced this injured relative—relative indeed, no matter how distant and how thin were the tie of the blood.

"Envy is a devilish vice, Gus," said Holden. "You couldn't endure that I should steal sixty thousand dollars and take it

141

away to enjoy by myself. You wanted to have my life, and that stolen money afterward."

Gus merely scowled. Then, looking around him to make sure that only these two could overhear him, he muttered: "Boys, let's not be foolish. I've got a pretty good chunk of coin laid away not seven miles from here. Take me into town and that money rots. Gimme a chance, and you get that coin. We'll split it three ways."

"How did you make so much money, Gus?" asked Holden quietly.

"Farmin'," snapped out the other. "How else would I be makin' it?"

"Some people," said Holden, "are so very lucky that they don't have to work, really, for their money. They simply ride out—at night, you might say. And when they come home their pockets are full."

"That's smart," said Gus, shrinking a little, and drawing his long frame down onto a stone beside the fire. "That's mighty smart, but it don't mean much—not to me!"

Holden smiled down on him. "You're a brave man, Gus," said he.

"Sure," sighed Gus. "I guess that I got my share. But—"

"Well?"

"What d'you mean to be doin' with me, Cousin Tom?"

"Chris!" said the cripple sharply.

"Yes?"

"Tie this murderer and coward hand and foot!"

At that, Venner leaned above the wretch, but from the throat of Gus there rose suddenly a long, wavering yell of terror and shame.

"Tom," he said, "for heaven's sake don't go bearin' malice agin' me for what I might of done to you in the old days. I never knowed what sort of a man you might be."

"But when you found out, you took a gun and came trailing me to—"

"I was gunna shoot it into the air, just to give you a start— because you was campin' out in the open, sort of."

"I heard the noise of that bullet you fired, into the air," said Holden. "You can say what you please, Gus. But remember that everything you say will come to the ear of the judge before many days."

142

"The judge?" breathed Gus. "Tom, Tom! You ain't carryin' it as far as that?"

"I am," said Holden.

"For why?"

"Not for my own sake, even though that counts. But I remember the way your father and you have treated my mother. If I could sweat you in purgatory for that, I'd do it."

"There ain't nothin' much agin' me," said Gus. "Not much. I say I was tryin' to play a joke on you. You say that this here was a try to kill you. Well, let the judge decide. Leastwise, they wasn't no harm done—except to me!"

Holden shook his head. "It won't do, Gus," said he.

"Why won't it do?"

"I know the whole truth."

"You lie!" screamed Gus.

"I don't lie. Ask Venner if I know. This is Chris Venner. Maybe you've heard of him. I imagine that he wouldn't lie about a thing like this. Ask him!"

"Well?" whined Gus to Venner.

"He knows enough to hang most any man," said Venner darkly. "I guess he'll do what he likes with you or most anybody else. What I mean to say, Curtis, is that I'd rather be in hell safe and sound already than have this here Tom Holden take after me."

"Eh?" asked Gus. And he surveyed the stalwart form of Venner, whose mighty hands he had so recently felt. He looked in turn at the slender body of the cripple. It was a mystery, and like all mysteries, it loomed mountain high before the ignorant fellow.

"What d'you want me to do?" said Gus suddenly. "What you got me here for?"

There was no answer. Venner, in pity, as the silence endured, opened his lips to speak, but Holden raised a hand which silenced him.

That deadly silence continued. And what has such a mortal sting as sheer silence, when an answer is needed?

There was not a word, not a sound. Only the fire kept up a subdued, murmuring conversation, dying branch to branch, and now and again the wind sighed heavily from the upper trees. The air had grown cold on their backs; the fire was hot in their faces; and big Gus, looking wildly into the flames, was working aimlessly at the ropes which bound him.

"Tom," he whispered at last.

His spirit was broken. Venner, in shame to see a human so subdued, started up and strode away from the fireside. But Holden did not stir. He himself had suffered too much. And all pity had grown small in his soul.

"Tom," repeated Gus, "you don' mean that you'd stand by and see 'em—hang me?"

"Why not?" said Holden coldly. "Why not? I'd see them break your neck, and I'd smile while I watched it! Why else did I set the trap for you here?"

28

AFTER THIS, for some time, poor Gus Curtis remained passively by the fire, trembling or perspiring, as different thoughts swept through his wretched soul.

He said at last, tentatively, like a frightened child: "Tom!"

Holden turned to him, and taking off his glasses, his clear, cold eyes looked through and through the other.

"Tom, tell me what to do. You was always smarter than me —at school work."

"You were always smarter than I—at fist work, Gus," said Tom.

Gus put up a hasty hand, as though to shield himself from that accusing thought. "I been a skunk," he whined.

"You knew," said Holden, "that everything you did while you were murdering and robbing near Larramee has been laid on my shoulders?"

"I heard something. I wasn't quite sure—"

"You lie!" said Holden.

That whip stroke turned the other white and silent.

"You hoped that you could keep it up and in the end have all the blame for it smash me, Gus."

Gus shook his head. He dared not speak. And he turned his eyes vaguely into the dark, as though searching for big Chris Venner. Any company was to be preferred to that of this cold devil of a cripple.

"But finally," said Holden, "when you heard that I had stolen a great sum of money from Venner, you were taken in and you decided that it was better to have my cash than to have me alive as a scapegoat. So you took up my trail—"

"Tom, I swear to heaven—"

"Be quiet," said Holden slowly. "I see your black heart, Gus. I've always seen it. I've always despised you as much as you've hated me. You've been a poisonous snake all your life. You'll be one until they stretch your neck in a noose. Do you understand that?"

For an instant, blind malice wrinkled the long face of Gus; then he remembered his helpless position. He said not a word.

"However," said Holden, "all that you've done for yourself is to win, in the end, the reputation of a despicable coward—a skulking rat, killing secretly—"

"That's a lie!" shouted Gus. "I fought 'em fair and square a lot of the time. I stood right up to Marshall and his kid. Old Marshall, he had the first shot at me. And I finished 'em both—" He paused, staring, pale, realizing how much this confession meant. Holden, scanning the darkness behind, made out the bulky figure of Chris Venner.

"Did you hear, Chris?" he asked.

"I heard," said Chris calmly. "I heard how he fought *square*, as he calls it, with an old gent of seventy years. I guess I heard as much as a judge would want to know!"

The head of Gus fell on his chest. He was seeing the hangman's noose already dangling before his eyes.

Afterward, Holden spoke apart to Venner.

"Partner," said he, "it seems to me that you and I together have nothing but good luck."

"My luck," said big Venner mildly, "is follerin' you and doin' what you say, Holden. Did I tell you that I spoke to Julie?"

"Did she send you away? Did she tell you never to come near her again, Chris?"

"It was just the way that you said it would be. She didn't do nothin' but get tears in her eyes about me while I was tellin' her how I raised the devil with other gents. D'you mind that?"

"Ah," said Holden, "one never knows what to expect from them. But usually, Chris, they go by opposites. If you know exactly what a man would think and do, then you can often come pretty close to what a woman will do by finding just the opposite. She cried over *you*, then, because you had rough-housed other people?"

Venner grinned sheepishly. "It was a mighty funny thing to watch," he declared. "I couldn't believe what I was seein'. I told her how I'd croaked one gent and stuck up another. What d'you think she said?"

"I don't know," said Holden, sighing. "What *did* she say?"

" 'You poor boy!' says she, and throws her arms around my neck.

" 'Wait a minute,' says I. 'I got worse to tell you, about how I up and robbed a bank, Julie—'

" 'Hush!' says she, 'somebody might hear!'

" 'It was a terrible crime,' says I.

" 'Nonsense,' says she, 'no doubt they was all rich people that had money in that bank. They deserved to lose it.'

"Holden, how could she come to talk to me like that, and her one that never broke the law in her life?"

"I thought she would be that way," said Holden. "Most good women would make very excellent crooks—for the sake of their families."

"Tom," burst forth big Venner, "how come you to know all about this? And the other things—where did you learn it all?"

Such was his attitude that if Tom Holden had declared a fiery angel dropped from heaven and whispered revelations in his ear, Chris Venner would have believed without question.

"I learned," said Holden, smiling, "by sitting and watching so long and so quietly that people forgot I was there."

At this, Venner scratched his head and then shook it. He could not understand.

"What are you gonna do with that rat, yonder?" he asked.

"You'll take him along for me."

"I'll be mighty glad to do it."

"Take him to Larramee. Take him to Mr. Oliphant Larramee himself."

"You don't know the rich man, do you, Tom?"

"I know him," said Tom, smiling again, "better than he knows me. Will you take Gus Curtis there?"

"I'll take him to hell gate and back, if you want," said Venner. "Will I find you there?"

"I'm coming to the town later. I'll have some one with me who'll need slow riding. Will you take care of Gus?"

A spasm of darkness crossed the face of the big fellow. "I'll take care of that square fighter," he said. "I'll bring him in. Maybe livin'. Maybe dead. But I'll fetch him to Larramee."

"You've done a lot for me, Chris."

"Me? My heaven, man, don't talk that way. You've stopped me from bein' a fool crook. Which I ain't smart enough to make money going wrong. You've made me so much coin that I dunno what to do with it. You've paid back the money that I swiped and got started on to the same bank that I swiped it from, and you done it in such a way that they'll never know that I copped the coin that day. Then you showed me the way to talk everything out with Julie, so's they'll never have to be nothin' concealed between us. That's some of the things that you've done for me, old-timer. And it's enough!"

Five minutes later he was riding through the hills rapidly, with Gus cantering a horse in the lead. And Gus was riding freely, without a rope to bind him, handling his own spurs, his own reins, his own quirt. He was held in check only by the slender noose of a lariat which was fitting around his waist and ran back to the horn of Venner's saddle.

In this way they journeyed on steadily through the night until the dawn came; and a little later, while the light was brightening, they came out on a ridge and saw, in the hollow beneath them, the long, winding street of Larramee. At this, though it was so early that there was not a stir or sound of life except the noise of the chickens and the moving of their hurrying bodies in the yards—though there was not even the lifting of a single smoke column above a chimney mouth, Gus Curtis cowered in his saddle and turned a fear-yellowed face to his guard.

"Venner," he breathed, "I dunno that I can stand it."

"Stand what?" asked Venner brutally. "That cacklin' of the chickens?"

"I'd rather get a slug of lead through my brain right up here and now!" stammered Gus Curtis.

Venner, with a snarl of scorn, raised his revolver, but as the black muzzle yawned on him, Curtis screamed and tossed up his hands.

"No, no," he pleaded.

Venner slid the long gun back in the holster. "I didn't know that gents come done up to look like men but really bein' nothin' but rats inside. I didn't know that folks could be like that. Now get on with me!"

147

He turned aside from the town and went toward the house of Larramee. It was a long circuit through the hills to get to the big ranch house without riding through the town, but Venner had pity on the cowering fear of his prisoner, and brought him by the long way. So it was the first brightness and the first heat of the morning when they reached the ranch. There on the lawn, as the two turned the corner of the roadway, Venner came suddenly on Oliphant Larramee walking with his daughter and with Mr. John Cutting, all looking marvelously fresh and gay and at ease with the world, so it seemed to big Chris Venner.

They stared at this apparition of victor and captive. Larramee stepped forward to meet the pair, but Cutting stayed behind with Alexa.

"Not quite as wild as the coming of the crippled murderer," said Cutting. "Still, spectacular enough."

"Who are you, my friend?" they heard Larramee saying.

"Me? I'm Chris Venner."

"And this man you have in the noose?"

"His name is Curtis."

"Are you an officer of the law, Venner?"

"Me and the law have got on tolerable well without leanin' none on each other for support," declared Venner.

"You have done this on your own account?" asked Larramee, smiling at the unwillingness of the other to come to the point, but equally confident that there was a reason behind this strange visitation.

"Nope," said Venner, yawning and then beginning the careful manufacture of a cigarette.

"You're working for some one, then?"

"You might say," answered Venner, unperturbed.

"Sort of an odd-jobs man?" suggested Larramee.

"Sure," grinned Venner, and they nodded at one another in mutual understanding, mutual appreciation. "I was sent up here by my boss."

"Ah? And why?"

"I don't ask no reasons. I do what I'm told to do."

"Perhaps you don't know who this long fellow you have with you may be?"

"I've a pretty good general idea. He's the gent that's been cuttin' throats and stealin' wallets around Larramee for a month or so."

148

"In the name of heaven!" murmured Larramee, "do you mean—"

He did not need to finish the question, for the terror of guilt which flashed across the face of cringing Gus Curtis, would have damned that man in the eyes of any jury in the world. One glance was enough to hang himself.

"It's a lie," stammered Gus, recovering himself. Then, feeling the disgust and the wrath in the eyes of the watcher, his own look fell to the ground and his chin sloped to his breast. He had felt the whip, and his spirit was broken.

"You were sent with this man, after you captured him—"

"I didn't capture him."

"Who did, then, and who on earth could have dictated you to bring that murderer to my house?"

The answer came suddenly in the ringing, strong young voice of Alexa from the rear.

"Tom Holden!"

29

NEVER DID AN audience of four greet such a remark with four greater attitudes of surprise; the prisoner jerked up his head and his hollow eyes glared terror and blank confusion upon the girl. Oliphant Larramee himself spun on his heel and shook his finger at Alexa.

"Don't be foolish, my dear!" he said almost sternly. "You've let the dread of that rascal become an obsession in your mind which—"

"He? That wretched little blinking rat!" exclaimed John Cutting, breaking in, in spite of courtesy. "Besides, he couldn't—"

Here there was a second interruption. It came in the huge, rolling voice of Chris Venner. "Gents," said he, "I dunno what the ways is around these here parts, but mostly where I come from, when a man has a partner, he sticks up for him when somebody up and sticks a knife in his pal's back. Gents, I aim to do that for Tom Holden."

Oliphant Larramee was actually embarrassed and surprised. And in many years his daughter felt that she had never seen him so moved as he was upon this occasion.

"You mean to tell me," said the rancher slowly, "that Miss Larramee is correct?"

"That's what I say," said Venner. "The lady is plumb correct when she said that it was Holden."

This brought a little sharp gasp from Alexa. She caught at the arm of Cutting, and he supported her, perhaps with unnecessary strength.

"Very well," said Larramee. "Your man, there, was captured by your dearest friend, and your dearest friend is no other than the peculiar—er—cripple—Tom Holden?"

Chris Venner did not like several things about this speech. He was so irritated by the entire interview, in fact, that now he lost all his awe of that great name of Oliphant Larramee which for years had been synonymous through the countryside for wealth, generosity and wisdom. He yanked his soft-brimmed sombrero lower, until the steep black shadow descended like a curtain across his eyes. Through that shadow he scowled down at Larramee, and between thumb and forefinger the cigarette which he was smoking dissolved into a shower of tobacco crumbs and morsels of paper.

"Mr. Holden," said Chris sharply, "is the gent that took in Gus Curtis. Mr. Holden, I dunno that I got the right to say that he's a friend of mine. Leastwise he's done more for me than the rest of the world put together has ever done. Mr. Holden told me to take this here poison rat and bring him to you. He talked like you would understand when I come up with this gent. But maybe you don't. And if you don't, I'll slide right along to the town with him. Talk up, Mr. Larramee!"

Mr. Larramee was compelled, first of all, to clear his throat. "Alexa," he said, "you need not stay!"

"Not stay?" cried Alexa. "Why, Dad, this is the most exciting thing that has happened in months!" And she came straight up and stood in front of Chris Venner. Perhaps some vague foreshadowing of an understanding swept across the brain of Chris, at that moment, as he stared down to the fresh face and the clear eyes of Alexa. What made him first think of it was her smallness, the marvelous smallness and delicate precision with which her body was constructed, compared

150

with the ample scope, the bone and the hearty substance of Julie Hendricks. This blue-veined wrist of Miss Larramee—even infancy could not parallel that. His emotion, as he looked at her, was equaled by one other thing alone, and that was the singular awe with which he was often overwhelmed when he found himself in the presence of Tom Holden himself.

"I'll stay," Alexa was adding. "I want to know a few things. I want to know whether—"

"Whether," broke in John Cutting, spinning his cane, "Mr. Holden, as you so precisely call him, is not himself the actual murderer and thief that has been troubling the vicinity—"

Mr. Cutting might sometimes interrupt. But he was not accustomed to interruptions, and he stared, now, as the heavy voice of Venner overwhelmed his own.

"Stranger," he said, "I dunno your name. Mine is Venner. Chris Venner. I allow myself to be the friend of Holden. And them that want to call him names, has got to do it when I ain't around, or else—"

"Or else what?" asked Cutting, who had plenty of courage.

"Or else I start to work on 'em," stated Venner. "Any way that they—"

"John," said Alexa, "please don't answer him, or there'll be a fight. And you're not a Holden, you know, to win fights by miracle."

"Holden? Bah!" cried Cutting.

The big brown hand of Venner dropped to the butt of his gun and then swung slowly away again; but thereafter, his glance was never long away from the face of Cutting, and his fury was easily legible in his eyes.

Alexa, however, came still closer. "Tell me," she said suddenly and gravely, "about your friend!"

"Alexa," commanded the father sharply. "I think you may go to the house."

"One moment, Father, please. Tell me, Mr. Venner, is he truly honest?"

Venner stared wildly about him. "Do I look honest to you?" he said at last, pointing to the stiff, strong arch of his breast.

"That's why I've asked you."

"Lady, he's as much more honest than me as I'm honester than that yaller skunk here beside me."

151

"Will you believe that, Alexa?" cried Cutting.

"Of course not!" said Alexa.

And she hurried away to the house. Her father watched her go, rubbing his knuckles thoughtfully across his chin.

"Is there any call for me and Curtis to stay up here?" asked Venner.

"None at all," answered Larramee. "Except that I'd like to ask you a word or two about this same hero of yours—this Holden."

"Mr. Larramee," said the big man, "me bein' short on words, that's one thing that I ain't gunna talk about. We'll let that drop and lie, sir."

So he left Larramee and rode down the hill, still with the rope fixed around unfortunate Gus Curtis. As for Larramee, he went back to the house slowly, his head down, his pace slow. He was not thinking of the prisoner or of big Chris Venner, or even of Holden; and as he stepped into the doorway, he heard a sharp confirmation of his suspicions.

"Alexa has gone up to her room," said Cutting, coming toward him. "This affair gave her such a shock that she wants to lie down a while in the dark."

Larramee nodded and went out from the house almost at once. He crossed to the western side of the building where he could look up at the window of Alexa's room. The shade was not drawn; and even as he stood there, looking up, he saw her come into the square frame of the casement, staring out across the hollow and the town which carried her father's name.

At this, Larramee went hastily to the stables. Twice he paused on the way and turned back to the house for a step or two, but each time he went on. He had them saddle a strong-limbed brown gelding, and on his back he stormed down to the town and straight up the road until he drew his rein in a cloud of dust before the house of Miss Carrie Davis.

She herself was in the garden; and even her stern face grew a little pale as she saw the great man, the great enemy, come upon her. There was no time to retreat with dignity; and to do anything without becoming dignity was far beneath Miss Davis. She folded her arms, therefore, and the only sign she gave of nervousness was the irregular waving of the trowel which was still grasped in her stout right hand

She neither advanced to meet Mr. Larramee nor retreated

152

from his coming. And now she saw him throw open the gate; she watched him lift his hat; she traced with a keen eye a new touch of gray at his temples; she admired again the brown, strong, handsome face; she observed the long, easy stride of an athlete; and as he came nearer, she was most unnerved to mark in his eye that same twinkling light which sometimes glimmered in the eyes of Alexa in her most bewitching moods. The heart of Aunt Carrie swelled; a lump choked her throat; therefore her frown was doubly black!

To this meeting after so long a disagreement, Mr. Larramee advanced, with a smile as bright as though he were greeting the nearest of friends. But Carrie Davis pressed her lips together. She wanted to be gay and debonair, as he himself was, but all she could do was to glower upon him. He went to the point with his usual directness.

"I've come to surrender," said he, "and beg you to talk to me about Alexa."

"And what?" snapped out Carrie Davis.

He was a bit staggered by this counter thrust. "And a mutual acquaintance of ours," he admitted. "That harum-scarum, strange imp of the perverse—Mr. Thomas Holden."

He saw that she was shaken by this; she did not reply at once, and he went on smoothly, to tide over her indecision.

"I've seen precious little of her lately, and she's been coming down to your house quite often."

"Do you think," said Miss Davis, "that she never comes to see me except to talk about men?"

He smiled broadly. "Of course not. But somehow, this chap Holden is in the air. Every one is talking about him, you know. The whole town buzzes about nothing else. And today a mountain giant came riding in with a captive to show me, and it seemed that Mr. Holden had sent him. He acted, by Jove, as though he were very happy to be a sort of messenger boy for the cripple."

"That is his misfortune," said the lady. "I wouldn't reproach him with it. Of course I've heard that Tom caught the sneak who has been raising Ned and letting the blame fall on Tom's head. Is that what you mean?"

"I mean," said Mr. Larramee, "that my daughter is a romantic girl. I don't know just how to put it—yes, I do know. I can talk frankly to you, I thank heaven. Miss Davis, I'm frightfully worried. Young John Cutting has been at the house for many days. As fine, clean-cut a youngster as ever walked. But Alexa doesn't seem to see him. She's abstracted. About what? Perhaps you know? Perhaps you'll tell me?"

"Do you think?" cried Miss Davis.

"I don't dare to think. I only know that in the offing is this young cripple, this odd devil who seems to be able to tame wolves and horses and"—he added, looking directly at her— "people, just as he pleases."

"It isn't possible!" cried Miss Davis.

"She hasn't talked to you, then?"

"And yet," murmured she, "why not? He has everything that a gentleman should have, except money."

"And name and background and—er—" Mr. Larramee stopped.

"Does it really matter?" asked Aunt Carrie.

"A cripple? An unknown vagrant suspected of—I don't know what?"

"I have nothing to say," said Miss Davis, and looked past her visitor to the pale blue sky.

30

ALL THE NIGHT Holden rested on the site of his victory. The next morning he began traveling slowly on and after many pauses, came at last in the first dark of the night to the cabin of Joe Curtis. He had purposely delayed his advance for the very good reason that he wished the news of what had happened to Gus to come to the cabin before him. He arrived, in fact, in time to find three kindly neighbors telling the event to the father, sitting eagerly about and drinking in his shame and his grief.

Outside the window sat Holden and watched and listened, while Curtis raged through the room and tore down a rifle from the wall, and then dropped into a chair and sat quivering, with his head in his hands. After this, the three looked to one another and went away.

As their horses scampered away down the road, "Judith!" called the big man.

And Tom Holden's mother came to the kitchen door, timidly, her tired head canted to one side, squinting her wearied eyes at the tyrant, and wiping her wet, red hands on her apron.

"He's gone and done it," groaned the owner of the house, not looking up to see that his call had brought her, so familiar was he with her slavish obedience.

"Who?" ventured she.

"Who is him that never brought me no luck? Who's the one that's never made nothin' but trouble in this here house? Your boy! Your brat! Your Tom!"

"Tom!" whispered the mother. "Ah, what's come to him, poor lad?"

"Hell and fire!" thundered the other. "Are you gunna pity the skunk that's landed my Gus in jail with a noose dog-gone nigh fixed around his neck already?"

Holden waited for no more. He went to the open door and stood there, stroking the long head of Sneak. Then he pointed, and Sneak went forward on his belly, gliding, noiseless.

"I ain't gonna have your face around to look at and remind me of what your brat has done. You can—"

"Cousin Joe!" cried she. "You ain't gunna throw me out where—"

"I've fed you here year on year. I've give you house and clothes—"

She pointed to the much-patched, faded wrapper which she was wearing. It had been blue gingham; it was a dull gray now with much washing.

"I ain't had a stitch, Joe," she said softly.

"Complainin', are you?" bellowed the big man, lifting a chair and crashing it against the floor. "What I give you ain't good enough? What I—"

"Merciful heavens!" cried Mrs. Holden.

He whirled to the direction which her frightened eyes indicated; and there he saw the wolf dog stealing on him. And behind the dog, framed in the doorway, saw the slender body of Tom Holden, with a great blue-barreled Colt hanging down from his right hand Mr Curtis grasped the rifle which was on his knees, dropped it again, and leaped back into a corner with

155

his hands above his head, his monstrous hands, which touched the ceiling above him as he stood there. And the flicker of the open fire made his face black and red by turns.

"Call off that dog—that wolf!" groaned Cousin Joe. "I'm an old man—I'm a father, Tom. You ain't gunna try to murder me like—"

"Turn your face to the wall," said Tom quietly, and as the other obeyed, he turned to his mother. So confident was he that the giant would not dare to stir, that he even embraced her.

"Do up the things you need. Not too much, because we're traveling tonight," he told her.

She looked at him in a bewildered way. "But what home—" she began.

"I'll provide the home and do the worrying about it," said he. "Now go along and bring down what you need."

He watched her hasten from the room, shaking her head but too much accustomed to obedience to even question him. Then he went back to Cousin Joe and stood close behind him.

"I've thought this thing over, back and forth," he said. "And I've had a hard time deciding. At first I thought that nothing would ever satisfy me except to flog you with a blacksnake until you crawled up to my feet and begged me for mercy."

He added, sharply: "If you stir like that again, Sneak will put his mark on you. He's a very nervous dog, Cousin Joe. He hates hasty movements."

There was a groan from Cousin Joe.

"But after all," went on Holden, "I decided that it would be for the best, perhaps, to let you go on as you have gone in the past. Let you live here, but without my mother to cook for you and slave for you and keep your house without pay and without gratitude. And without your son to take a pride in; your true son, Cousin Joe, a coward like you, a bully like you.

"Sometimes, when I think this thing over, I wonder what under heaven is so fearful a poison to the world as the sight of a creature like you living in it and calling himself a man. There's nothing very greatly worse, I suppose. Nothing very greatly worse, sir! What a gift to society to remove you, like a stain from a clean white page. A touch of a knife, or a touch on a trigger would do the work so neatly. It would be so soon

156

over. And the whole range of the mountains would be easier because of it.

"However, death is too easy. You have to have pain. A worm that will bully a woman—a weak woman made helpless because she has a child to take care of, a crippled child at that, well, well, Cousin Joe, I had better not think about it or talk about it.

"Now stay where you are, for I warn you, if you stir, Sneak will have you by the back of the neck. And I'll not be here to stop him."

For he heard, now, the tapping of feet on the stairs, and the creaking as his mother descended. Then she came out into the room with fear in her face, and an old bonnet, some twenty years out of fashion, but ridiculously new and bright, on top of her head with a red feather sticking up from the one side.

The cripple looked at her with a heart breaking with amusement, pity, love, and sorrow. For what if Alexa should see her in this array?

But he took her inside his arm. How very small she was! Smaller, even, than Alexa, and her poor back bowed with long labor. He kissed her forehead, he kissed the smile that was trembling on her lips, and led her out into the night.

At the copse he brought out the red stallion.

"Dear heavens, child!" cried she, clasping her hands. "Do you expect me to ride that monster?"

"He will be as gentle as a lamb to you," said the cripple. "It's only the strong people in the world he hates and dreads. There'll be nothing for you to tremble at, I promise you!"

She could not help but believe him. And she could not help but sigh as at last she sat aloft in the saddle, holding fast to the pommel.

"Ah, Tommy dear, look at the sky! I'd almost forgot that there was stars!"

Holden looked up to her, smoothing the neck of the stallion. It was really most wonderful. He had expected some trouble, at least, but there was not a stir of great Clancy. He merely tossed his head and pricked his ears; and when he stepped away, with Holden hobbling before him down the road, he went as softly as a lamb.

Then Holden whistled. A short howl answered him from the house. Sneak came like a gray bolt from the rear and shot away into the lead. All through the night he circled about them, cutting far ahead, and then to the side, and then falling to the rear, to report anything which the nose of a wolf might find and which the brain of a man might recognize as an enemy.

But there was not a thing. The night lay quiet about them. The wind was breathless in the trees. A broad moon, deepest orange, at first, came up to light them, then turned to white and rolled through the black of the heavens where all the stars went out.

"It's the beginnin' of a new life," whispered Mrs. Holden.

But her son thought of Alexa. "It's the end of everything for me," he told himself. "And yet, what hope did I have, after all?"

31

A DOZEN TIMES every hour he changed his mind and made it up again. They slept at a little town twelve miles from the house of Cousin Joe. And when they wakened the next day, he finally reached his decision in the gloom of the morning, when the mind of a man is only half his own.

He decided that he would scorn a sham. He would enter Larramee with his mother dressed in this same ridiculous costume, perched high in the saddle on great Clancy, with Sneak for their bodyguard. Let the world laugh at him—if it dared!

So thought Holden, like a sulky boy shaking his fist at the whip which is about to strike. But when he came to the top of the hills overlooking the town, his heart failed him. They would see with such bitterly critical eyes. And the secret smile behind their hands, how could he endure that?

Yes, some one might laugh aloud, and when he wanted to destroy the offender, he would be powerless, for, after all, there was never a moment of the day or the night when he was not conscious that all of his strength was a gigantic pretense, a huge sham!

He had gone too far to turn back now, however. So down the hill he went, working hard with the staff, exhausted by his day's march, and he came into the main street to be greeted with a whoop of exultant laughter by a dozen youngsters who instantly gathered around him. They dared not laugh aloud, when they were close, but their snickering behind his back was incessant. And Holden, his face pale after the first burning, went slowly on down the street. Clancy grew skittish in the uproar and began to dance, so he helped his mother down, and they walked side by side. Surely as absurd a pair as ever walked elbow to elbow!

"What is the matter with those children?" she asked him.

"They're glad to see us, that's all," said he.

Jeff Carter, the cow-puncher, came by with a companion, stopped to stare, and then rolled in their saddles with laughter of the silent kind as Holden went on down the street at the side of that bobbing, ridiculous red feather. Others came out to their front porches and to their windows to observe. The whole town seemed to know instantly, as though the big black crow which was constantly croaking around them gave a warning of their coming.

"Tommy," said his mother, "they're laughin' at something. I don't see nothin' wrong with you. Is there something wrong with me?"

"Not a thing in the world," lied Holden bravely. "And here," he added, "is the house of a friend of mine. And there she is in the garden."

He paused at the gate, groaning inwardly, but forcing a smile. "Miss Davis," said he. "I've brought my mother to town with me to keep house, d'you see? I want you to meet Mrs. Holden."

He watched Aunt Carrie's eyes widen over the red feather, the old, bedraggled clothes. Then she dropped the watering can with a crash, kicked the trowel from the redbrick path, and advanced with the broadest of smiles, stripping off her man's stiff gauntlet glove as she came. She took Mrs. Holden's hand and smiled, indeed, but with such tenderness that the head of Holden spun. He could not understand.

"Come in," said the witch. "You must be tired out, poor Mrs. Holden."

"I'm fair to middlin' petered out," admitted Mrs. Holden.

"But I get along. I tell my boy that I ain't much tired by nothin' while I have him along with me."

The witch blinked a little at this vocabulary and at this grammar, but she took Mrs. Holden in hand at once and guided her into the house.

"An old friend of mine is here," said the witch in her loud voice, as she opened the door and brought Mrs. Holden in.

Holden himself paused in the doorway, bewildered, shocked. For he guessed what had happened. Alexa was there; and the witch had brought in his mother in that ridiculous garb only to show her to the girl, that they might laugh about it, afterward.

"Close the door, Tom," said Aunt Carrie.

"Is she here? Alexa?" asked Tom with his lips.

"Close the door!" cried the witch. "Half the dust in the town is blowing in on me!"

He obeyed, and as he trailed on after them, he saw her standing up from a chair—Alexa in a riding suit, with her crop still in her hand, and wonder still in her eyes as she recovered from the first glimpse of Mrs. Holden. But after that, while the witch was introducing them, and while Holden was nerving himself desperately to encounter terrible Alexa's blue eyes face to face, he discovered suddenly that he had ceased to exist; for in that room there was only one concern, whether for Alexa or Miss Davis, and that concern was the little old woman with the red feather in her old-fashioned hat. Too much attention they seemingly could not pay her.

And while Miss Carrie Davis prepared coffee in the kitchen with her accustomed lightning dexterity, the beautiful Alexa, in the front room was sitting close beside Mrs. Holden, chatting in the gayest possible manner, until Mrs. Holden herself forced attention upon her son.

For she said: "Dear Miss Larramee, I'm a glad woman that my boy has fallen in with such good friends; and him never no sort of a man to pick up friends among girls!"

Poor Tom Holden could have shrunk through the back of his chair, but behold, Alexa turned upon him a smile so frank and so radiant that no one in the world could ever have guessed that there might once have been a cruel scene between these two. One might have sworn that they were old friends!

And what was she saying?

"We are all very proud to have Mr. Holden in our town, Mrs. Holden. Because, you know, every real town needs a giant killer, don't you think?"

"Dear Miss Larramee," said the old woman, raising a work-roughened hand, "I dunno how all this talk about Tom and fighting could of started. Because I know that he never had a gun in his hands all the days of his life; and as for ridin' a hoss, he was hardly ever in a saddle. Books was all his life. Books, books, books, till I used to think he was bewitched. And now they tell me that he's a fighter; and that big strong men are really afraid of him. Well, I would be seein' that before I'd believe it. Though he has changed a mite; bein' a lot browner and more cheerfuller now than I ever seen him, dear boy!"

And turning to Tom with a motherly smile: "Fetchup your necktie a mite tighter, Tom. It's all askew."

Poor Tom was utter crimson, now, and dared not look at Alexa saving from the remotest corner of his eye; and he found that she was in a brown study, frowning and scrutinizing him. He felt that he was more lost than even he could have expected. And if he felt no resentment against his poor mother, it was because he pitied her as much as he pitied himself.

But the gloom of the fair Alexa ended in a moment. Then she was chatting as gaily as ever; and when the coffee came, she had to pass sandwiches to Mrs. Holden and pour her coffee with her own hands. And, then would not Mrs. Holden take off her hat for the sake of growing cooler?

Mrs. Holden answered: "It's real kind of you, ma'am. If I ain't botherin' you none——"

And off came the hat, revealing a broad, smooth brow beneath, sharply cut across by the red incision of the hat's lower edge. Holden breathed a little more freely. Surely, unless they were blind they would see the eternal goodness in those mild eyes and in that timid smile, and in the whole shrinking form of the little woman.

"Get me some fresh flowers for that vase yonder in the corner, Alexa," said Miss Davis in her most dictatorial manner.

The beautiful Alexa arose with a smile and went into the garden.

But what was this?

"Tom Holden!"

"Yes?"

"Are you blind, man?"

"I don't know—" began he, at a loss.

"You act like it! Let a girl go out alone into a garden to pick flowers and dirty her fine hands among weeds and—what not?"

"Miss Davis—" he began.

"Bah!" said she. "Go out there this minute!"

32

SHE SPOKE WITH such withering severity, that little Mrs. Holden winced and looked from one to the other to make out whether or not they were really in the midst of a bitter argument. Tom stood up, slowly, leaning heavily on his staff.

"Maybe Tom's a mite tired, walking all those miles!" said the little mother, creeping feebly to his defense.

The witch struck that feeble protest brutally to the ground.

"Stuff!" said she. "That man's as strong as a giant. He can do what he wants to do, and that's as much as the best giant could do in any fairy story. Tom Holden, go out there and help her pick flowers!"

So Tom limped across the room, and just outside the door he stood for a moment leaning upon his staff and trying to fortify himself. For this was far, far more awful than any ordeal through which he had ever passed in his life. This was more dreadful than that frightful moment during which he had faced Crogan through this same doorway. Because in that time of stress, Sneak had come beside him to help, just as Sneak came now, with wicked little eyes on his master's face, trying to read the mind and the need of the human.

But Sneak was no help now. There was no place for a brute intelligence here! He drew a great breath, therefore, looked pitifully down at the dog, and then hobbled down the steps and up the gravel. Alas, how clearly now he could remember Alexa dancing in the schoolhouse, like a windfloated feather!

She was in a corner of the garden, where a tree sprinkled the ground with a black patterning of shadow; she was on her knees, stooping over some little red flowers with yellow throats. He had not the slightest idea what they might be termed. And he wondered, vaguely, why one should pick such short-stemmed blossoms to fill so large a vase as that which the witch had pointed out to the girl!

His shadow fell across her.

"I think these will do, Aunt Carrie," said the girl, and then she looked up and saw Tom and opened her eyes in surprise.

"Oh," said she, "is it you?"

"It is I," said Tom, feeling his own insufficiency more terribly than ever, and yet wondering in his heart of hearts that her absorption in the picking of the flowers had been so great that she had not heard the noise he made dragging down the path—so unlike the long, light step of the witch! And indeed, no matter how intent she had been upon her work, she had not as yet plucked a single flower!

"May I help you?" he asked, with the gentleness of one who expects a refusal.

At this, she looked up to him again.

"I suppose so," she said critically. And forthwith she rose.

How gracefully, how lightly she moved! And he labored down upon his knees, lowering himself down the staff like an old man!

"Are your eyes very sharp?" she asked him.

"Does one need to be very keen?" he asked her.

"Of course. You want the young flowers."

"How does one tell that?"

"And you a great woodsman? A great trailer?"

She stood over him, laughing. "I'll tell you. The older ones are just a little wrinkled at the very lip of the petals. Can you see which is which now?"

He took off his glasses. He leaned a little lower. "I think I can make them out," he said, eager to succeed.

He began to pick them. A little silence came. At last he held up a hand half filled with fresh young flowers.

"I think those will do," said he hopefully. "Do you think so?"

To his immense surprise he found that she had dropped her chin upon a doubled fist and was staring down at him, and not at the blossoms. It was an attitude which she had copied, no doubt, from that excessively mannish Miss Davis, but what was mannish in the witch was only the more delightfully girlish in Alexa.

"Is there really no malice in you?" she asked sharply of him.

"I don't know what you mean," said he very truthfully.

"About the house; the way I treated you; and John Cutting striking you—"

"I deserved trouble," said he. "I was very presumptuous. And I've wanted to explain, you know, that I never really—I mean that what I said—it was rumor that mixed up everything and made such a mess. And then I didn't know how—because it was all so—"

"I'm sure," said Alexa, "that I don't know what you're driving at. I don't understand."

"I'm not a bit good at these things," said Holden. "I'm trying to apologize, because—"

"Why did you bring her here?" asked Alexa.

"My mother?" he asked huskily, turning white.

"Yes."

"She's very alone without me. She is happy with me, I trust."

"And you?"

"I?" said he, somewhat through his teeth. "Of course, I'm happy with her! Of course! Besides—"

"Well?"

"I didn't want to pretend," said he rapidly, looking down at the flowers and making a vague attempt to pick them, and a very unsuccessful attempt at that. "People were saying very odd things about me. You know, some one said that I came out of a rich family in the East and—" He paused.

"Do you understand?" he asked her. "I wanted every one to know exactly what I was; and what my mother is. I should not want any one to—er—respect me—who couldn't respect her. It's rather hard to explain—"

"Your glasses don't seem to be much help to you," put in Alexa.

He was glad that the subject was turned. "I suppose that Miss Davis told you about those?" He smiled at her, in a conciliatory fashion.

"Not a great deal. I don't believe she ever did, in fact, mention them."

"That was another pretense. They aren't glasses. They're just window glass."

"But why on earth?"

"They made me look a bit older, don't you think?"

"Heavens!" said the girl.

At this he flung them hastily away. They clattered and broke on a rock far off.

"I didn't know that they looked as bad as that," he explained, coloring.

"Oh no! I didn't mean to be rude, Mr. Holden. Except—oh, well, there's no way to say it. Only, I'd like to ask you a question."

"I shall be delighted."

"Will you tell me the real truth?"

"Oh, of course."

"You promise?"

"I do," said he, very solemn.

"Did your mother tell the truth when she said you'd never used guns in your life?"

That interrogation struck him with a shock. There were a dozen men who hated him; there were scores who would be glad to add to their reputations by shooting him down if once they really knew that he was helpless with weapons. He could not speak for a moment. He could only watch her in a dull, hopeless fashion.

"It's a dangerous question, in a way," he said. "But—I have to confess. It's true."

"Thomas Holden!" cried she.

He pulled himself up by the staff and stood before her.

"Do you mean," she went on, "that you faced Crogan—and did those other things—without being able to actually use a gun?"

"I—"

"And that you went out after the murderer, Curtis, and caught him, and brought him back, without being able to shoot—at all?"

"You see—"

"And that that huge big man with the bad temper—that monster Venner, was so afraid of you on account of nothing at all?"

He shook his head. "There are tricks," he admitted sadly.

"And that was all?"

"That was all."

Every instant he was growing hotter.

"I saw you and I heard you brave down John Cutting."

"He had heard foolish things about me. Really, there was nothing else for me to do. And—"

"All sham!"

"You see," he urged bitterly, "God made me weak. I've loved strength. I've worshiped strong men. I've forgiven brutes who hurt me, just because I believed in their right to be cruel so long as they were powerful. But I was always the way you see me—something to be despised. I've despised myself more than other people could. Will you believe that? But finally I saw that in order to live, even, I had to pretend to be something that I wasn't! I had to pretend to be clever, and witty, and wise, and very, very brave!"

He dared not look up to her face at all, by this time; but he studied the pattern of the path and wished himself yards deep beneath its surface.

"And you're nothing of all these?" snapped out Alexa.

He shook his head, and sighed.

"Not even brave?"

"I have to tell you the truth. I'm not. Not really brave, Miss Larramee. It was all bluff. I've been frightened almost to death, by Crogan, and riding Clancy—"

At that instant the horse, as though he had heard his name spoken, lifted his head and neighed from the street. The girl looked out at the splendid animal. Then she looked back at the crippled form of the master.

"It's almost too wild to be listened to!" said she.

He could not answer.

"A dozen men, if they guessed, would want to murder you, Mr. Holden!"

"I hope not so many," said he very faintly.

"More, more! Why did you tell me?"

"You asked me."

"You're walking on the edge of a precipice with nothing but sham to hold you up?"

"I suppose that's it."

"Heavens!" said the girl.

And Holden felt that the world had ended.

Here a window slammed up.

"I can't wait any longer," said the cross voice of Aunt

Carrie. "If you haven't found the flowers I want, come in, anyway."

They hurried in. The girl was much ahead of Holden, and as she passed through the door, Holden heard her whisper to the witch: "Thank you!"

For what, he wondered? For calling her in and ending a painful interview, perhaps? He was more ready than ever to die!

33

HE TOOK MRS. HOLDEN to the store, first, and there she bought a simple dress. Then he got her a pleasant room in the hotel where he found the energetic Mr. Jefford of the Larramee *Tribune* waiting for him. He wanted a story, and he wanted it very badly. He wanted to know about a great many things. He wanted to know, among other things, about the affair at Maybeck; he wanted to know something about the quiet little woman who was the mother of the hero; he wanted to know above all if there were any chance of the great man settling permanently in the town of Larramee and whether that old rumor about—a certain lady—

Here he was rudely checked by the cripple.

"At least," said the editor, growing a trifle despairing, "you'll have some statement about the reward?"

"What reward?"

"What reward, Mr. Holden? Why, the eight thousand dollars for the capture, of course! Or—don't tell me that you didn't know about it! But Gus Curtis confessed everything today. The sheriff broke him down!"

"Who pays the reward?" asked Holden.

"The sheriff himself."

So Holden went to the sheriff. He was given a very gloomy reception. The officer of the law paid over the eight thousand with no apparent joy.

"Young man," said the sheriff, "you're lucky. About the luckiest I ever seen in my life. I've been wirin' to Maybeck to see if old Julius would make a charge. But dog-goned if he don't refuse. He won't hear of no arrest nor do action agin' you. Young man, what did you do to hypnotize old hard-headed Julius Maybeck?"

"I," said Holden by the way of answer, "want the name of the nearest good lawyer. Or do I have to go to El Paso to find one?"

"El Paso the devil!" said the sheriff with much local pride. "I aim to say Judge Kiernan is the slickest lawyer in the whole West, bar none! He could prove that red was black any day!"

Holden went straight to the office of Judge Kiernan and found a fat little man with a cigar which he held in his teeth in the center of his mouth and talked around it and stared with reddened eyes through the mist of stinging smoke.

"What could keep Curtis from hanging?" asked Holden.

"Worrying about that?" asked the judge. "Well, son, the only thing that could keep him from hanging is me. And he won't get me."

"Why not?"

"My price is too high."

"How high?"

"Five thousand for a man-sized job like that."

"Here is eight thousand dollars," said Holden.

"You want me to help the district attorney put a rope around his neck, Holden? You want to make *sure* that Curtis doesn't get off with a prison sentence?"

"I want to make sure," said Holden, "that he isn't hung."

"Why, in the name of heaven?" asked the lawyer, blinking.

"Because blood is thicker than water. He's a cousin—a good many times removed from first. Will you take the job? Eight thousand if he gets no more than life. Nothing if he's hung."

The judge did not hesitate. He took a firmer grip upon his cigar and then swept the money into a pocket.

"The state'll have to pay for his board. It's all settled," he said.

And Holden went back to the hotel; on the veranda he encountered none other than the great Larramee in person.

"Young man," said the millionaire, "I've come to invite you to my house for the night. That's according to agreement."

Holden shook his head. "We'll let that go," said he.

Larramee frowned at him. "How's that?" he asked to make sure.

"Make it something else. When I can ride a cow pony," and here Holden smiled faintly, "I'll come to ask you for a job. Will you hire me then?"

Larramee lighted a cigarette and inhaled a long puff thoughtfully.

"My lad," said he, "you've beaten me twice, against great odds. Confound me if I don't think that you could beat me again. I want to do you a turn which may mean a good deal to you and which I can manage without much effort. I'd like to finance you to the East. Say, to New York. And in that city I'd pay the doctor's bills when they take a look at that crippled leg of yours. Some of these modern specialists work miracles. Why not on you?"

"You are a thousand times too kind," said Holden. "And what must I do in return?"

"A very simple thing. You merely keep away from the state. Forever!"

"Is there nothing else?"

"Not a thing."

"I think," said Holden, "that you need not make the offer. I believe that I'm to leave the state very soon."

So he nodded farewell to Larramee, and went on into the hotel.

34

THERE WAS NO sleep for Holden that night. And he was up by the dawn. At breakfast time he met his mother with completed plans. They were to start north in a buckboard and meet whatever chance brought to them. So he left Mrs. Holden busy getting things together for the trip, and he himself went to say farewell to Aunt Carrie Davis.

He found her in the kitchen doing her breakfast dishes and talking amiably to a large yellow cat which was curled in the morning sun that burned across the window sill. She showed some confusion at the sight of Holden, peering through the screen door at her.

"You might whistle, man," she told him, "to give a body a thought that you're comin' dashing in on 'em. What will you want at this hour of the day?"

"I have come to say good-by," said Holden.

"Good heavens," cried the witch, "the man is mad!"

"I have come to say good-by," said Holden, feeling that she must have misunderstood him.

"I'm not deaf," said she. "You've come to say good-by. Heavens, what a great fool a young fool can be!"

He waited a little. But she strode over to the window with her mannish step and stood there looking forth upon the country. She was so filled with peculiarities, that for all Holden knew, this might be her way of saying farewell. So he replaced his hat on his head and turned away. The witch knew by the sound, without turning her head. "Come back here," said she. "Come back here and listen to me."

She continued to speak without turning to face him: "I see what you are, young man," said she. "You're one of those that hang about and flatter a woman until you've unsettled her heart. And the minute she's concerned about you, you fly away to some other place."

"What woman?" asked Holden meekly.

"What woman, you rascal?" cried the witch. "Why, what but lovely Alexa?"

Never in his life had Holden moved so fast. He did not know how he managed it. But somehow he was inside the screen door, and tall and trembling before the witch.

"You are saying this to torture me!" breathed Holden.

"Bah!" said the witch. "No man understands what true suffering can be. However, be off with you, now. You've said good-by. Begone with you."

"Alexa—" stammered Holden.

"She'll get over it. Time is the best cure. It's just your queernesses that have turned her head. Any girl is taken by oddities. Poor Alexa! Thank heaven that you are leaving!"

"Did she tell you—"

"That she thought you were a madman. However, I think that she's right. Good-by, Tom Holden! Don't come to another woman with your lies the way that you've come to Alexa Larramee!"

"But does she—may I—" stammered Holden.

"I'm a busy woman," said the witch. "I can't be talking my morning away. I think maybe Mr. Larramee will be sorry to see you go, too."

"What!"

"He made a trip all the way to Maybeck and talked to Julius Maybeck about you. He says that he can't understand what you've done to Maybeck. He's ready to believe that you could do almost anything, young man. Now run along with you. I'm a busy woman!"

With this, she turned her back on him, and Holden went through the screen door, not softly, however, but with a wild stare in his eyes as of one who sees a vision in the broad light of the day. He hobbled forth to Clancy. He climbed into the saddle upon the lofty back of that giant of horseflesh. Then he loosed the reins and Clancy fled up the road and then whirled along the hill and plunged onwards to the house of Larramee.

Presently he stood before the door. And above him came the lofty form of Oliphant Larramee himself.

"You've come to see Alexa, I suppose?" said he.

"Yes," said he faintly.

"And what the devil do you propose to say when you see her?"

"I propose to tell her that I—worship her," said Holden.

"Bah!" said Larramee. "And what are your future plans in case she's as great an idiot as you could ever wish her to be?"

"My future plans, sir, I have not thought about."

"You have a mother to take care of, I believe?"

"Yes."

"And do you think that you could make shift to carry the burden of a wife, as well? Or do you plan on receiving help?"

"Mr. Larramee," said Holden with a sudden flush in his face and in his mind, "I shall be delighted to take every just burden that comes my way. As for my ability to carry the weight, it does not even bother me!"

Larramee stood back with a sigh. "Alexa is in the library yonder." said he. "I think she saw you coming up the hill. and she half expects you, I believe."

Holden, his head spinning, advanced across the floor to the lofty, arched doorway which connected the broad living room with the higher, more Gothic library. And there he found Alexa, far back among the shadows, a shadowy form herself.

171

"I have come to tell you—" began Holden.

Then he found that it was impossible for him to utter a sound in his throat. He closed the door softly behind him.

Afterward, a full two hours, Mrs. Holden grew restless at the hotel. For it was not the way of Tom Holden to be dilatory, and she had inculcated in him habits of punctuality. An hour and a half ago, at the latest, he should have returned. But he did not come. So she schooled herself in patience for the period that followed. Finally, she went from the hotel and up the street.

She had only a single resource. That was in Miss Carrie Davis who had been so kind to her the day before. She might be able to tell her what had happened to Tom.

She found Miss Davis apparently under a cloud, for she was far less hospitable than she had been on the evening before. She had seen Mrs. Holden's son, she admitted, but she did not know where he had gone. Yes, she could guess, but she did not care to reveal that guess. It was all too ridiculous.

"What," said Mrs. Holden, "is ridiculous, Miss Davis? What has Tom done?"

"A wonderfully foolish thing," cried Miss Davis. "Something, however, that might be expected from a silly dreamer like Tom!"

"Do you think he is so very silly?" asked the mild mother.

"Idiotic!" snapped out the witch.

Mrs. Holden, of course, was both crushed and silent. And presently she saw Miss Davis raise a bony hand to command further quiet.

"What do you hear?" she whispered.

"A horse galloping," ventured Mrs. Holden.

"Stupid!" said the witch. "Of course you do. But the point is—are there two horses or more than two running together?"

"Oh, half a dozen, I should say."

"Your ears are no good. There aren't more than three. There may be only two. There may be only—"

Here she paused and stiffened in her chair.

The hoofbeats rushed up the street and came to a sudden pause—exactly in front of the house of Miss Davis.

"I'll go look—" began Mrs. Holden.

"Don't stir!" cried the witch. "This is a fairy tale. It isn't true. If you stir, everything will melt into thinnest air. Listen!"

Footfalls came up the walk. Two pairs of feet, and a

172

grinding thing upon the bricks, like a cane ground down with a great weight.

"It's Tom," breathed Mrs. Holden, and she smiled so radiantly that a faint brightness came even across the withered features of the witch.

"And who's with him?" asked the mother.

"A blessed angel," said the witch, "has come down to him. That's why this story isn't true at all!"